The Diplomatic Bag

THE DIPLOMATIC BAG

ANOTHER SPY THRILLER

BY PETER MARSHALL

This book is published by PMA (London and Washington DC)

All rights reserved, including the right to reproduce this book or portions thereof in any form whatsoever.

No part of this publication may be reproduced, stored in a retrieval system or transmitted in any form or by any means, electronic, mechanical, photocopying, recording or otherwise, without the permission of the publishers.

Copyright: © Peter Marshall 2024 (www.petermarshall.uk)

Cover design: © Nick Goodman 2024

Paperback ISBN: 9798344748641

Imprint: Independently Published

PROLOGUE

In my first four spy novels, I created a series of individuals who carried out the shady and hazardous activities around the world of the British MI5, America's CIA and Russia's FSB. Some of my fictitious 'spooks' perished ... but others remain active and continue their work in this latest story. But now they also have to confront the challenges which come with the emergence of new technologies. The national security agencies are making crucial changes to meet a new world order – including international coordination.

Meanwhile, beneath the surface lurks the continuing use (or mis-use) of the time-honoured "diplomatic bag", which has its origins in an earlier era.

In the UK, MI5 is the governmental agency responsible for security and counter-intelligence, together with its sister organisation MI6 which operates around the world to stop terrorism and disrupt activity in hostile states. A third key operation is GCHQ, the government intelligence and communications organisation.

Then, in the United States, the CIA (Central Intelligence Agency) is tasked with gathering, processing and analysing national security information from around the world and taking action through its Operations Directorate. It is mainly focused on intelligence gathering overseas. Alongside the CIA is the FBI (Federal Bureau of Investigation), which is the domestic security service.

In Russia, it is the FSB (Federal Security Service), which is now the country's main internal security and counter- intelligence service (but still commonly known by its previous abbreviation GRU). It is also one of the successor agencies of the Soviet-era KGB and is responsible for anti-terrorism and military surveillance.

All the characters and their activities in this story are fictitious – with the exception of Frank Gardner, the BBC's remarkable radio and TV Security Correspondent, who I have included as a tribute to his real-life example (as you will read in chapter 2).

Finally, I must add that once again, I am indebted to "anonymous" friends with relevant experience for their comments and insights as they read drafts of this story for me. I hope the end result will prove to be enjoyable for readers, as well as thought-provoking.

Peter Marshall, Torquay, Devon, 2024.

CHAPTER ONE

The New Chief

It was 7am, an earlier than usual Monday morning start for Alistair McLaren, the newly-appointed Director General of MI5, Britain's counter-intelligence and security agency. He was still adjusting to the greeting at his front door by an armed security officer – with a formal "good morning, sir!". Then, in the official, black bullet-proofed car, he was driven from his recently rented apartment in the smart Primrose Hill area of North London to be ahead of the traffic congestion to the agency's Thames-side headquarters.

On the way, at the start of only his second week in the new job, he had time to review the latest updates and messages on his high security mobile tablet. Fortunately, there were no new weekend crises to distract him from the first task of the week – a live radio interview after the 8am news on the "Today" programme with the BBC's security correspondent, Frank Gardner. So he only needed to make a routine call from the secure car phone to his assistant, Melanie, already at her desk in the top floor executive suite.

"Hope you had a good weekend?" he began. Assured that all was normal for a Monday morning, he continued: "When the BBC people arrive, they can set up the interview in my office – it's just radio, by the way, not TV cameras. And remember that Frank Gardner may need some help with his wheelchair".

Melanie, calmly efficient as always, confirmed that she understood and her new boss then added: "By the way, would you also keep an eye open for Patricia Wells in the operations section. She should be there by 8am as usual and I would like to see her in my office straight after the BBC interview – and before the usual Monday staff meeting".

It was only one month earlier that Alistair McLaren had accepted the unexpected promotion to the top position at MI5 in London after serving for three years as the Deputy Director at GCHQ, the UK's intelligence, security and cyber agency. Tall and elegant, with a serious demeanour, he had been identified as a high-flier after gaining a first-class degree in cyber-technology at Oxford University. His career began as a trainee at an international bank in London, but his university record quickly led to an offer to join the Civil Service. His first government job was in the technology development section at the Home Office, before being promoted and moved on to join the MI5 agency as an intelligence analyst. After two years there, he successfully applied for a more senior position as a section manager at GCHQ, another UK Government facility 100 miles West of London near the city of Cheltenham. It has some 5,000 staff housed in a large, modern circular structure (known as 'the donut'), some 100 miles west of London. Its activities are secret and wide-ranging and they include monitoring worldwide communications.

During the next 10 years at this high-tech operation, McLaren's outstanding abilities earned him a series of further promotions, eventually becoming deputy to the organisation's Director General. It was his reputation as the impressive number two which now earned him the appointment by the UK Foreign Office to return to London to head MI5, the key security services organisation. At the age of 41, he was now the youngest person to hold this key post, succeeding the retiring veteran of the operation, Sir Charles Bentley.

His promotion and move to London had been suddenly accelerated by the news that the former Director of Operations at MI5, Tom Spencer, had been murdered, together with his new wife Marina, during a relaxing holiday in the Scottish Highlands. A device had apparently exploded underneath their car when it was parked in a remote village at a country inn.

Like Alistair McLaren, Tom Spencer had risen rapidly through the ranks of the UK security services and had headed the Operations Section at MI5 for more than ten eventful years. He had recently married and taken the opportunity for a well-earned early retirement. The tragedy in Scotland sent shockwaves throughout the British security community and his former colleagues quickly recognised that the double murder had the hallmark of a 'revenge hit' by the FSB, Russia's Federal Security Service which implements government policy for national security, counterterrorism, and the protection and defence of the Federation.

As details of the tragedy began to flow from Scotland to MI5 in London, an initial review of the evidence confirmed the initial assessment of a terrorist action. Images from the one convenient car park security camera revealed that two men had apparently planted a device under the couple's flashy white Lamborghini which had exploded when they returned to their vehicle after a pub lunch and started the vehicle's ignition. The loud explosion had shocked a dozen or so local residents, some inside the pub and others living nearby and they had responded quickly to the deafening noise. But they could do nothing to help when faced with a blazing car and flames which had also spread to other vehicles parked nearby. They could only wait helplessly while their '999' calls brought the nearest police and emergency services at high speed on the narrow mountainous roads to the village in about 10 minutes. There were soon three uniformed police officers on the horrific scene in such a lonely and usually peaceful spot. They were soon followed by an ambulance team and then the fire service truck. But all that could be seen by these first responders was the still-smouldering, burned out vehicle and it was clear that there were two occupants who were beyond any help from the medical team. At least two other cars parked at the pub were badly scorched and damaged beyond recovery.

The senior of the three police officers took control and quickly recognised that this was an incident for the experts in the criminal investigations department from the nearest city, Aberdeen. After sending his initial report, the instructions from CID were for the area to be sealed off as a crime scene and also to start making discreet inquiries in the pub and the village to try to identify the two victims. Also, they were told to seek any information about strangers seen in the village that day?

Some 15 minutes later, a detective inspector and his CID team landed by helicopter from Aberdeen at the village school playing field. They took one look at the incident and recognised that there was no way to help or to easily identify the two victims. But they were able to see the car's registration plate when they viewed the video recording from the car park security camera. These details were rapidly identified by the police team as belonging to one Thomas Spencer at an address in London. Also, because the initial evidence pointed to the use of an explosive device, the CID detective decided that it was a matter to be reported urgently to the security experts in both Edinburgh and London.

Within a few minutes, the name of Thomas Spencer had been recognised at MI5 headquarters with amazement and horror and the senior officer on duty placed an immediate blackout on any information – a message which was quickly passed to those on the scene in Scotland.

The security camera playback had also shown that two males, wearing dark overalls and disguised with woollen hats and scarves, had arrived on the scene in a plain white van. One man could be seen approaching the Lamborghini while the other kept watch. The first man was then seen carrying an object from their van to the far side of the white sports car, and then returning a minute or two later – and the van drove off at speed. It was assumed that their plan must have included their escape route from the lonely spot in the mountains. Accordingly, immediate alerts were sent to police forces in Scotland as well as to airports and ferry services throughout the UK to be on the alert for two, probably foreign, individuals and the white van.

The local inquiries made by the police officers revealed that the victims were known to some of the villagers as Thomas Spencer and his wife. They had been visiting his brother Bernard who had lived in the village for a few years and some of the locals had been introduced to them by Bernard when they had met briefly in the pub a few days earlier. It was understood that the two visitors would then be staying at the house there while Bernard and his wife were travelling oversea, pursuing his career as a well-known undersea cameraman making TV programmes. Very little was known locally about "Tom and Mary", as they had introduced themselves to locals, except that they were 'very nice people' – and the main subject of conversation had been their "amazing white sports car".

Further investigations by the police revealed that the remote Scottish house had been inherited jointly by Tom and Bernard from their late parents and was a perfect base for the younger brother to relax between his long overseas filming trips. The owner of the village pub held an emergency mobile phone number for Bernard and this time, his travels were interrupted by the dramatic news from the Scottish police and they made a hurried plans for a return trip from the latest assignment in Alaska. When the couple eventually arrived home two days later, there was little they could do to help the inquiries. They were there for the inquest in Aberdeen, which was opened and then adjourned after hearing outline evidence about the incident from the police and the post mortem report on the two victims. The Coroner's verdict of 'murder by person or persons unknown" enabled Bernard to go ahead with arrangements for a quiet funeral for the couple in the village church where their parents had been buried after living there for many years.

The news of this tragedy quickly reached a shocked Alistair McLaren at GCHQ in Cheltenham, and his planned move to MI5 in London was accelerated. He faced an immediate new challenge to fill a double void in the leadership of the key agency. During his first week in the new job, there were a series of sombre meetings with the top staff as new details of the incident flowed in. They all remembered the years which Tom Spencer had spent there, bringing his special skills and energy to the tasks they faced.

At such a difficult time, the new boss specially appreciated the support and advice of his predecessor, Sir Charles Bentley, who had worked closely with Tom for many years and had thoughtfully changed his own retirement plans to remain in London until Alistair settled in. He decided to avoid returning in person to the MI5 headquarters, but he was able to meet his successor discretely at his nearby London club in the evenings for invaluable handover advice and also to share reminiscences. Crucially, to maintain operational continuity, Sir Charles had already appointed Gordon Livesey as Acting Operations Director until a permanent successor to Tom Spencer could be appointed.

Gordon was now close to retirement age, so he was unlikely to be a candidate to succeed to the Director role. But his long experience as a top intelligence officer, former agent and prodigy of Tom Spencer, was invaluable as the inquiries progressed ... not least in developing secret plans to ensure that the ruthless double killing would be matched by an appropriate response against Russia.

Gordon and his operations team quickly focused on assembling a full record of the recent activities and contacts made by the newly-wed couple. Tom's new wife, Marina, had also served as a secret agent and the research soon showed details of how, most recently, Tom had been making a world tour to British embassies to say farewell to many of those he had worked with over the years; and meanwhile Marina had been winding up her final and highly successful assignment for America's CIA agency in Japan. The team began to examine the records of all the secret operations each of them had been involved in during the past two years, with details of any contacts made by them, particularly relating to their Russian adversaries.

And during this unexpectedly challenging first week at MI5, another of Alistair's tasks in his new role was to start the sad but formal process of finding a successor to Tom Spencer in the crucial senior role as his Director of Operations. During these long and busy first days, he was impressed by the team supporting Gordon Livesey at this difficult time, and in rare quiet moments, he developed an important new plan for the agency's future ....

CHAPTER TWO
A BBC Interview

Soon after talking to her new boss from his car, Melanie had a call from the reception desk at Thames House to tell her that "the BBC people have arrived". She asked the duty receptionist to arrange any help they needed and then took the lift down to the ground floor to bring the visitors up to the top floor Director General's office. In the spacious and impressive lobby area she prepared to greet them and to her surprise, it was just two men – one was leading the way, carrying two small equipment boxes.

"Hi - I'm Jack, the engineer," he said warmly, as she introduced herself as Melanie, the DG's assistant. Then she greeted the other man following behind slowly in an electric wheelchair. She quickly recognised him as Frank Gardner and had spoken to him a couple of times by phone in the previous week, after he had called her to request an interview with the newly appointed DG. To her surprise, Sir Alistair had agreed to the suggestion - after consulting his Whitehall bosses. This was unusual for such a normally secretive part of the Government, but the BBC man's reputation had earned him this positive response.

Frank Gardner had worked as a banker in Saudi Arabia before deciding to try broadcasting for a new and more exciting career. He based himself in Yemen and began to cover news in the Gulf area as a freelance before his appointment as the BBC Middle East correspondent, based in Cairo. He went on to travel widely through the region, specialising in defence and security issues, until June 2004 when he was involved in an attack by al-Qaeda sympathisers in Saudi Arabia and was shot six times and seriously injured. His cameraman was killed, but Gardner survived thanks to major surgery, firstly in Saudi and then back in UK.

After a total of 14 operations, 7 months in hospital and many more months of rehabilitation, he returned to reporting for the BBC using a wheelchair or a walking frame. In spite of these limitations to his mobility, he again began to travel widely and enhanced his reputation as an accomplished BBC security correspondent, working for radio and TV news programmes. It was his expertise in this role which earned him the positive response when he made his bold request for a live interview with the newly appointed boss of MI5.

Melanie took the BBC team up to the Director General's stylish, modern office suite where she suggested they use the glass-topped conference table at the end of the room to conduct the interview. Within a few minutes, they had organised two microphones and she heard the engineer setting up the digital link with the Today programme producer at Broadcasting House studios. When the DG strolled in calmly just after 8am as planned, they were already listening to the prior subjects covered in the flagship morning news programme, which had been on the air for a couple of hours. Frank Gardner breathed a sigh of relief as he was greeted warmly by his interviewee, who was friendly and relaxed. After a few minutes of reassuring conversation between them, the BBC engineer gave them a 'thumbs up' and said their microphones were now live. Then they heard the anchorman's introduction:

"We now have a noteworthy event as we go over to the headquarters of Britain's secret services in London for the first live interview with the new head of MI5, Alistair McLaren. At 41, he is the youngest Director General in the history of this crucially important organization and he started as its top man just a week ago. So over now to MI5 on the bank of the Thames in London where he is with our Security Correspondent, Frank Gardner".

Gardner's experience had prepared him well for this occasion and he began by congratulating the DG and asking about his background and the experience he brought to MI5 from his previous role at GCHQ. The new DG began his reply with a warm compliment to his interviewer on his amazing recovery from the life-changing incident in Saudi Arabia. He then went on to describe how he had started his own career as a researcher with an international bank.

"It was not really my scene," he added, and went on to explain how he was then recruited by the Civil Service and began in the communications department of the Home Office. He became a section manager responsible for monitoring covert intelligence sources. A year later, he successfully applied for a research job at MI5, where he worked for two years until his transfer to GCHQ in Cheltenham as an intelligence analyst.

"I realise you cannot talk too much about your activities at either of these agencies", was Gardner's cautious follow up. "But you were soon promoted to senior level and then eventually to the number two role as Deputy Director. These must have been challenging times with all the new technologies expanding their reach around the globe?"

"Yes, it certainly was," came the reply. "The agency had been tracking these changes for years of course, but among other things and because of the pace of change, I created a new section which I called Group 2030. Their objective was to forecast the likely impact of changes in terrestrial and space technologies during the next decade on a global basis – and to consider how these developments would affect our mission to monitor information and intelligence".

With a smile and an audible chuckle, he added: "I am pleased to say that the new team worked so well that I had to double the budget and the number of staff in the group in the first two years."

"I am sure that was not easy", said Frank Gardner. "But I guess they were producing results which you probably cannot talk about in any detail today. But was it that success which has now brought you back to MI5?".

"I don't know about that," came the reply. "But I had been having some preliminary discussions about MI5 with government ministers, who were considering the retirement of Charles Bentley after his long career here. And then things were suddenly accelerated after the very tragic death of Tom Spencer. That was so sad".

"Yes, what a shock that was for us all," replied Frank Gardner. "So what happened next?"

Alistair McLaren gathered his thoughts and continued: "In meetings with the Home Secretary since my new appointment was announced, he made it clear that my brief here includes a clear emphasis on new technologies and seeking out how various uses of them might threaten our security here in the UK. Among them, of course, is the increasing impact of Artificial Intelligence, which also poses massive threats if it is misused. And of course, these are all global problems so I will be working closely with my colleagues in MI6 and among our allies on the international scene about these high-tech threats – which exist not only here on earth but increasingly in outer space as well."

Frank Gardner followed up, asking for more details about the successes to date in pursuing these areas. But the DG replied that as the 'new boy' he was still discovering what had already been achieved in recent years. And he went on to emphasise the impressive skill levels of the teams in both GCHQ and MI5 and his aim of "keeping one step ahead of the bad guys."

"Speaking of the bad guys," continued the interviewer. "Can I go back to the tragic death of

Tom Spencer and his wife? What else do we know about it now? Who was responsible?"

"Not at this stage," came the cautious reply. "This was a great shock to us all and it was clearly a terrorist act of some kind. The investigations are continuing on that basis and we will issue a statement later. I came to know Tom very well over the years. He had a highly successful career with a creative approach to the vitally important tasks he undertook and he will be long remembered for that."

As the interview came to an end, the anchorman of "Today" at Broadcasting House thanked Alistair McLaren warmly for his precious time and added that he was sure Frank Gardner would be reporting much more on the important work of the secret services in the future.

CHAPTER THREE

Call Me "Tricia"

Jack, the BBC engineer, signed off from his link to Broadcasting House, said thank you to Melanie and departed to the BBC car waiting outside, carrying the technical equipment. Meanwhile, Alistair McLaren had asked Frank Gardner if he could spare just a few more minutes. Getting a cautious nod from the reporter, who was looking at his watch, the DG buzzed his assistant and asked: "Can you ask Patricia Wells to join us here as quickly as possible?"

There was hardly time for more conversation about the success of the interview when the door swung open and to Frank Gardner's surprise, in came an attractive and smartly dressed woman in a wheelchair almost identical to his own. The astonishment was matched by PaTrisha who managed to gasp a muffled "well hello" .... and the silence was only broken by the DG who decided to make formal introductions, adding that he knew how much Patricia had been inspired by the recovery and return to work by the BBC correspondent. He then reminded Frank Gardner how Patricia had lost her mobility nearly three years earlier when she took a Russian assassin's bullet intended for her then boss, Tom Spencer, when they attended a function together in Portsmouth Dockyard. And in her case, it had been a Ricin poisoned pellet which led to complications and a long recovery.

"Yes, I do remember of course," said Frank Gardner. "It was a terrible shock and I remember how you took the shot intended for Tom. And now it seems they have got him in the end. Anyway, it is a real pleasure to meet you at last and also to share our experiences of losing our mobility like this. How did it affect you, if you don't mind telling me?".

Patricia collected her thoughts and explained carefully that the Ricin pellet had apparently damaged a nerve in her spinal cord and that she was so lucky to survive. She could see that the BBC man wanted to know more and she went on: "They told me afterwards that the Ricin had caused a multi-organ system failure which led to low blood pressure. Apparently, this was severe enough to lower the blood flow to my spinal cord and lower limbs. Somehow, the doctors were able to limit any further damage elsewhere, but it had caused enough permanent damage to require this wheelchair. So here I am, and kept going with regular physiotherapy and the wonderful people here."

"It is also wonderful to have you back at work" added the Director General, who continued: "Patricia has been a key member of the team here for several years and she learned a great deal from working as Tom's assistant. Now she has come back in stages during the past six months or so, rebuilding her career here very successfully".

"I am so pleased and really impressed," said Frank Gardner, warmly. "I hope we can find another opportunity to get together to share our experiences, but I really must go now ... it takes me a while these days to get to my next date. I will be back in touch, Patricia."

"I do hope so," she replied. "I have always admired your work and never imagined I would meet you in person, and certainly not like this."

They reached out from their wheelchairs to squeeze hands together. And Frank blew a kiss in her direction as he was led out by Melanie and taken down in the lift to rejoin his BBC colleague. Patricia shook her head disbelievingly and prepared to follow, but she was stopped by the DG who said he needed a chat with her. He went briefly outside to say his farewell to his interviewer and then returned to his own desk, with its view over the River

Thames and beckoned Patricia to move her wheelchair slowly across the room to join him.

"I have been looking at some of the reorganisation I need to do here to keep up with the changes in the outside world," he began. "It is just as I was describing to Frank – I assume you heard the interview?"

"Oh yes, we were all tuned in," said Patricia. "And we thought it went really well and touched all the right points. He is such a good reporter and he understands how far he can go with his questions, unlike some others I can name."

"Well, I am sure he will think he also has a good new contact here in the agency now," said the DG with a smile. "He will certainly follow up with you. But I think you now have more than enough experience here to handle that, which brings me to the reason for this meeting. I am told by the other directors here that since you came back here just six months ago, you have done some tremendous work investigating some of the areas I was talking to Frank about - new technologies and so on. As you know, we have just posted a notice for applications to fill poor Tom's vacancy as Operations Director and this has led me to think about the glowing reference which Tom would surely have written for you had he been here".

"Yes, he was such an inspiration," commented Patricia sadly. "I miss him enormously and most of the things I learned with him have been so valuable since I came back to work. And I cannot thank your predecessor enough for being so patient during my long recovery and also getting me restarted by working from home at first on those research projects."

Alistair then said how much he also appreciated the decision by his predecessor, Sir Charles Bentley, to delay his departure until he could complete the move from Cheltenham to London. And also how he had sensibly promoted Gordon Livesey, to be the acting Operations Director – knowing that Gordon, just two years before a well-earned retirement himself, would not apply for the vacancy.

"So in the circumstances, I guess it has worked out as well as it could so far," the DG continued. "And now I want to tell you about my plans. To begin, I have revised my budgets so that I can now appoint two new directors ... and I would very much like you to be one of them. I intend to create a new division here in MI5, very much on the same lines as my 2030 group at GCHQ. I guess you heard me describe it to Frank Gardner?

"Well, the challenge here of course will be rather different. We will not only need to research all the new technologies ranging from artificial intelligence to developments in outer space, but also seek out those areas which could be exploited by the bad guys to threaten our national security. So I am planning to create a new position of Future Development Director – and I would like it to be you. As I said to Frank just now, the future is really a global security issue and there will need to be close liaison by the new Director with MI6 and their contacts around the world. How does that sound to you?"

"That is quite a challenge, but I certainly understand the need." replied Patricia after a few moments of thought. But then she added confidently: "Yes, I think I can do it ... for Tom's sake as much as anything. And I must say that I find Frank's example of working from a wheelchair is so inspiring."

There was a tear running down her cheek as she added: "When do I start, sir?"

"Please call me Alistair," he replied quickly, adding. "And do you prefer Patricia or can I call you Pat?"

"I'm afraid that is a sort of family problem", she replied. "My brother was called Patrick and so he became Pat and this led all my close family and friends to call me Trisha. So would that be okay with you?"

"Just fine with me, Trisha" he said with a laugh. "And by the way, I had better tell you that I have had an official letter from the Cabinet office to tell me that I have been given an honour for my work at GCHQ - actually a knighthood which will be announced tomorrow.

"Well, that's marvellous. Let me be one of the first to say congratulations – Sir Alistair," she said as she turned and propelled her wheelchair from the office.

CHAPTER FOUR

Russia's Hit Team

At the glossy headquarters of the Russian FSB Secret Service in Moscow, Yuri Bortsov was still enjoying the satisfaction of the successful elimination of his long-time arch-nemesis Tom Spencer. At a meeting with his boss, the Defence Minister, together with other chiefs at the Kremlin, he proudly described how two of his best agents had slipped into the UK as tourists, unrecognised, and began the task of tracking down the recently retired head of MI5 operations.

He related in detail how his plan had started when one of their London-based agents had succeeded in discovering Spencer's residence in the city. The sleuths had then identified his spectacular white Lamborghini car and found an opportunity to attach a discrete tracking locator under the chassis. When the two killers from the Moscow-based hit squad arrived in the capital, they started following his movements in their small rental car and waited for an opportunity to carry out their assignment. They had been issued with the necessary weapons from the secret armoury store at their London embassy and on the second day of their close observation at the address, they reported seeing their target and his female companion loading their smart vehicle with luggage.

Bortsov went on to describe how his two chosen agents were ready for this unexpected departure by the couple and were able to follow them on the motorways, first to the North of England and then after a break at a convenient services area, they drove on to a remote village in the Scottish highlands - "they stayed on their tail for nearly 300 miles," he added with admiration and then he continued:

"They were able to report to me in a coded message that they had discovered the destination of their target as a large house in the village. So I authorised them to just wait for an opportunity to complete their objective successfully".

Bortsov went on to describe to his senior team how later the same day, the target couple had driven to a village hostelry, and this gave them the first opportunity to plant an explosive device under their parked vehicle.

"They sent me a 'mission accomplished' message", he announced proudly and after acknowledging the group's applause, he said: "And there is more".

He went on to describe how the two agents then began a complex escape plan which involved a fast drive through the mountains to a deserted and lonely farmhouse which had been discovered by their London-based team. There, they had abandoned their rented vehicle discretely and the agency's chief in their Copenhagen embassy was able to arrange a helicopter to meet them for the flight across the North Sea to a small Danish island. One of their most experienced locally-based agents at the embassy then drove to the chosen landing spot in a quiet national park area to welcome them back.

Bortsov concluded: "We are now waiting to get the news from Copenhagen that they are back safely from their successful mission".

The senior group again applauded the successful operation and a glowing Bortsov told his chiefs: "So it all worked at every stage. This was one of our most important assignments of the year and it went smoothly, including those last-minute changes in planning for their escape route. I think our guys now deserve to rest up at the Danish embassy for a few days and then make their way back to Moscow in stages. We will give them a hero's welcome at the Kremlin when they return - and a financial reward".

Later, at his regular meeting with senior staff back at FSB, Bortsov had more to say. He had been surprised to learn from his people at the London embassy that the death of Spencer had not received the expected level of publicity in the British media. They had been surprised that the incident in Scotland was never followed up by the press beyond one short news item in a Scottish newspaper about "two fatalities in a mysterious car fire at a village in the Highlands". It had identified the victims as being Sir Thomas and Lady Spencer from London on a holiday tour of Scotland and only added that "the incident is being investigated by the authorities." Then, he had learned that a routine obituary notice appeared in the London *Daily Telegraph* two days later, recording the career of "Sir Thomas Spencer, the recently retired and well-regarded former Operations Director at MI5".

Bortsov smiled and told his senior colleagues: "And that was all," adding with a chuckle: "We did a great job but did not get much credit. But that confirms that we have hit the British secret services where it hurts most and they have as much control over the media there as we do here."

Then turning to future planning, he continued: "So now we have a new top MI5 group in London to learn about". One of the most experienced member of his staff was Yazov Razovsky, and the Director chose him to give priority to working with their London-based resources and contacts to produce a full report on the changes at MI5 and MI6. He said he wanted to see detailed organisation charts and a report which included the profiles of the team now in place, together with their locations, duties and responsibilities and past history – with a first draft available in two weeks.

This challenge was welcomed by Razovsky, who was currently on a razor's edge for his career prospects. He had been highly regarded as head of the FSB bureau at the London embassy until he made a major error during the mission by the infamous agent known as the "Russian Lieutenant". This had resulted in him facing an embarrassing high publicity court case as an accomplice in the death of a British naval employee and he was sentenced to eight years in jail.

However, he was fortunate to be a convenient 'spy swap' participant when the wife of a prominent British businessman was detained in Moscow – and he was now back in the agency, working to rehabilitate his reputation as part of the secret service team. He was assigned to a role as an analyst, preparing reports for the

Defence ministry on counter-intelligence systems in western nations – but this was a task he regarded as "important but boring" after his years working as a senior intelligence officer, mainly in overseas embassies.

Razovsky confirmed that he fully understood the new assignment and said he would work with his former colleagues in London to assemble the required information.

As Bortsov ended the meeting, he called out to his assistant: "Let me know as soon as you get any news from Copenhagen and ask the monitoring unit if they have heard any more yet?"

CHAPTER FIVE

News From Denmark!

At the headquarters of America's CIA at Langley, Virginia – just a few miles from Washington DC – the experienced Chief of Operations, Bob Chivers, was at his desk early as usual and reading the overnight situation reports from his directors around the world. He paused when reading a 'top secret' message from his man in Copenhagen, read it again and then called to his assistant:

"Hey, get me that new boss in London on the hot line – what's his name, Alistair something, I think. I met him briefly on the line last week, so he knows who I am. And if he is having lunch with royalty, then interrupt him."

Within a few minutes, his assistant was back to tell him: "It is Alistair McLaren and he has only been there a week or two. He's on the line now."

"Good morning, Bob," came the crisp English voice. "It's good to talk to you again. You are up early so it must be important."

"You bet it is – and it's a follow up to the sad story you told me last week about poor old Tom Spencer," began the American spy chief. "So let me give you the latest. We have been closely monitoring the various message your people have been sharing with us about the terrible incident in Scotland. Well last night, our very smart bureau director in Denmark sent an amazing report – for my eyes only. It seems his people at our embassy are able to track coded secret messages coming out of Moscow and they followed up when they saw one sent to the Russian embassy in Copenhagen. It referred to two important people arriving direct from Scotland. Okay so far?"

"I am intrigued," came the cautious response from London. "Tell me more?"

"Well, if you are ready, it seems that our guys in Europe are pretty curious and the team at the Danish embassy started tracking everything coming across the North sea by ship and by air," he continued. "Then they picked up an unidentified helicopter approaching a deserted area in a national park not far from Copenhagen. They were suspicious and thought it might be linked with the terrible incident in Scotland. so our agency boss there sent a couple of our best hit men there pretty fast. Well, hear this. They reported arriving at the location just in time to see a helicopter departing. They also saw two pretty scruffy individuals there plus a young man with a car. They identified the vehicle as one we knew from the Russian embassy so our local director gave them the OK to hit. And that was enough."

"That's amazing work – sounds like the CIA at its best. So what happened next?" asked Alistair McLaren, quizzically.

"You don't want to know," replied the American caller. "Except that we are sure that this was linked to the search for Tom's killers. There was some sort of a challenge and resistance in the park and you can be sure that Tom's killers are no more. So just close the file and forget it completely, except perhaps with a quiet smile when you hear any squeaks from Moscow".

"That's quite a story, Bob", replied the new boss of MI5, slowly absorbing the surprising information. "All understood - and now I really know that I am working in a different world. Is there anything else while we are on the line together?

"Yes, when are you coming to Langley?" came the reply.

"I can't wait – I will give you a date as soon as I can and I look forward to sharing a bourbon or two with you," said the British chief, shaking his head disbelievingly as he replaced the red phone.

Meanwhile, in Moscow, a pensive Bortsov was still pondering a mysterious confidential message from the Russian Ambassador in Copenhagen to report that the expected arrivals from Scotland had just disappeared, together with one of their local agents who had been sent to meet them.

He immediately got the Ambassador on the line and asked him briskly: "What's going on?" He was told that further discreet inquiries were discovering no more information. They had sent a young agent to meet the helicopter but after getting one brief message to report that the aircraft was approaching the expected landing site as expected, they heard no more. There was simply no sign of the agent, his car or the two expected arrivals.

Bortsov replied: "Let me know at once if you hear any more. Otherwise say nothing." He put his head in his hands and worked out how to report this to his Minister. The mission to eliminate Spencer had been successful – but at a cost – and the less said the better. This news would not be welcomed.

CHAPTER SIX

The Diplomatic Bag

Yuri Bortsov knew all too well how the State Security business had to live with 'downs' as well as 'ups' - and at his next meeting with his departmental managers. There was no reference to the mystery of the team sent to the UK. He was in a positive mood as he told the group: "Today, I want to show you the latest equipment which has been developed by our technical team which could be very important."

He picked up his phone, hit a number, then said "Vasiliev? Are you ready? Then come on up to my office now and brings your toys with you?"

After a couple of minutes of suspense among the group, the experienced technician arrived and entered the chief executive's suite nervously. It was the first time he had entered the spacious offices on the top floor. He waited in the doorway until he was beckoned to join the group and then followed instructions to place what appeared to be a small radio on the table. "Ok, play us what you can?" asked Bortsov. A few adjustments later, they were astonished to hear the slightly muffled voice of their boss saying: *"I want to show you the latest equipment which has been developed by our technical team ...."*

"So how about that - we have been bugged," the boss told his astonished top team, and turning to the technician, he asked: "Now tell us what this is all about?"

Vasiliev then showed the senior group a black disc, the size of a saucer, which he described as part of a new technology just developed by their secret research team. He explained that it could be attached discretely to the outside of an office building to record conversations inside via micro-seismic vibrations of the structure. It used microwave lasers to accurately detect the movement of air particles - even through walls – and could then convert them into individual sound waves and conversations. These were then recorded on the small book-sized receiver they saw on the table.

There were mystified reactions around the table and replying to the questions that followed, Vasiliev explained that the black disc could be easily hidden in a crack in an exterior wall, or even the space between a window or door and the adjoining wall. The quality of the recording would be improved with further work, he said, adding that they were also able to link the device to a translation and transcription system which could rapidly produce a hard copy of the words it had recorded.

He explained how this system differed from others currently used by spies around the world and described the difference between radio waves and the development of laser beams designed to transmit sounds. This included the range of the signals and the ability to penetrate walls. He confirmed that for this test he had been in the parking space at the rear of the building and was able to locate their voices in the top floor office within 5 minutes.

After further detailed questions had been answered, Bortsov thanked the young technician who departed with his equipment. The Director then told his top associates: "That was impressive – agreed? So we are now planning to set up a further test in the Kremlin with a fake meeting taking place in the special briefing room which has silicon lining as protection against any external recording devices. Obviously, we do not have that protection here in my office. But Vasiliev's research director has assured me that this laser system can only be blocked out by other much louder noises. So we shall see?"

He went on to describe how he already had approval from the Minister to go ahead with a plan in which one of the technical team – probably Vasiliev - would go to the London embassy posing as a regular courier with a diplomatic bag which had the small laser units hidden inside. He would work with their bureau chief to choose a suitable location for a secret trial of the system in the field.

"Isn't it a bit risky to use the diplomatic bag for this sort of thing?" asked the experienced Razovzky. "I have seen a few of these attempts and they have had embarrassing consequences - or worse."

Bortsov laughed and waved off this comment - "Don't worry, we will take care of this and I am sure we are not the only ones using the bag for other things. How do you think the Chinese send their drugs to Europe?"

He then decided to reassure the meeting with a quote from the international agreement on the matter:

"A diplomatic bag usually has a lock or tamper-evident seal to deter or detect interference by unauthorized third parties. As long as it is externally marked to show its status, the "bag" has diplomatic immunity from search or seizure, as codified in article 27 of the 1961 Vienna Convention on Diplomatic Relations. It may only contain articles intended for official use."

In the discussion which followed, he told his top team that the Kremlin test would take place during the next few days and if successful they would go ahead with a more realistic field test of the system, probably in London. And as his colleagues looked at each other and then nodded their approval of all they had heard, he closed the meeting with a positive message: "This equipment could be an important breakthrough if it works in the real world. We will discuss it again when we have some more details of our plans".

CHAPTER SEVEN

Mysterious Signals

It was a busier-than-usual period at the headquarters of the CIA in Langley, Virginia. As well as the current agenda of investigations and missions around the world, there were new technology challenges emerging every day - particularly in Russia and the Middle East as well as in China and Latin America.

Bob Chivers, the Operations Chief, was at his regular review of the current priorities with his senior team when a top secret message arrived on his screen from GCHQ, Britain's international counter-intelligence and global monitoring service, which got his attention.

"Unusual laser signals identified today by satellite monitoring over Russia. Location near secret services headquarters in Moscow."

Chivers read it to his colleagues who were all mystified by the news and they were able to immediately confirm that the mysterious signals were not the work of anyone in the CIA or any other US agency. After a brief discussion, the chief then made a quick check call to his own monitoring services director at their headquarters in Texas. He read the confidential message and was reassured that whatever had been detected also had nothing to do with any US military or defence activity. He added that he would get his own experts to check it out.

"Okay, what action?", Bob Chivers asked his colleagues. "This may be a red herring, but I think I will take this opportunity to have another chat with the new guy at MI5 in London. They will have seen this message first so they may have some more details by now".

He called to his secretary, at her desk outside his office: "Hey, Josie, can you get me that new top guy in London again? Is this a good time to get him on the secure line?"

She reminded him that he was called Alistair McLaren – then added that she had just seen a report that he has received a knighthood and that now he was now actually "<u>Sir</u> Alistair". She added that according to an announcement received the day before, his title had been a reward for some successful work in his previous job at GCHQ. She also reminded him that Sir Alistair had replaced Charles Bentley, "who was also a sir". She then added that she would place the call immediately.

In less than a minute, the red phone bleeped and Josie said very politely: "Mr. Chivers, I have Sir Alistair on the line."

"Well, yes, hi, hello ... sir," stuttered the American, also recovering from the fact that his secretary had never before called him "Mr. Chivers".

"And good morning to you again," came the cultivated British reply. "I appreciated your earlier call which was a bit of a shock here. And I am sorry not to have called you to introduce myself before now, but these last few days have been rather hectic. And can I call you Bob? I feel I already know you from reading the files from all the work which you did with Sir Charles and with Tom Spencer of course."

"Yes, Sir Alistair, it is important that we continue to work together and I hope you are settling into the new job," he began, only to be interrupted: "Well, this news has travelled fast, even for the CIA, Bob, and you can forget the Sir – that's just for we Brits. So what's on the agenda now?"

"It is a message from your former pals at GCHQ this morning about laser signals in Moscow. I did an immediate check here and I can assure you that it is not anything which originates from us. What do you make of it?"

"I am glad you have seen it," said the MI5 boss. "We are mystified at the moment as well and we are carrying out some further expert analysis. What we do know is that it lasted just a few minutes and probably originated locally in Moscow. It could be some sort of test being carried out by the Russians? Or it could be some alien activity there in the city? And if so, by whom?"

"Thanks for that, Alistair, let's stay in touch", replied Bob Smithers. "And if you have another minute, can you tell me who is replacing poor Tom? That was a terrible business in Scotland and we all felt it personally here - not just Tom, but also Marina – they were both such great people and they deserved a long retirement together".

"We really appreciate your thoughts," said Sir Alistair. "It was the FSB of course, and we think we have now identified those who planned and carried out this senseless killing. And between you and me, your guys in Denmark probably made sure we never hear from them again. Anyway, we will let you know how things progress. I never actually worked with Tom myself, but he was a friend and colleague over many years as we both made our way in this business. He will be a hard act to follow, but I hope to be able to make an appointment as our new Operations Director in the next week or two and I will send you the details".

"I look forward to it," replied Bob. "And yes, I guess you will be looking at more ways to keep Moscow on edge and if you need any support from us, just give me a bell. Which reminds me, in case you did not catch up with it during your changeover there, we kicked out half a dozen Ruskie diplomats from their embassy here after they hit our Ambassador's home in London with a drone attack".

"Ah yes, I read all about it– that was a good move at your end and something like that may be on our agenda here," said Alistair, who then continued: "By the way, you may also like to know that we will soon have two new Directors here. I have decided to create a new position of Development Director. The job is to research all new technology developments likely to affect our work in the next 10 years and to prepare a long-term plan. And this post will be filled by Patricia Wells, who I think your people also knew as Tom's assistant".

"Wow, that's great news," said Bob enthusiastically. "Yes, I remember the name. I think we met her on several visits here and wasn't she the friend who looked after Marina when she moved to join us here as well?"

"Yes, could well be", replied the London DG.

Tom then continued: "And now, if I remember correctly, she is also the gal who took a hit last year from those Russian spies who were targeting Tom at an event in the UK somewhere. So what has happened to her since then?"

"She had a tough time," replied the MI5 boss. "It was a Ricin pellet intended for Tom, as you said. It caused damage to her spinal cord and it was touch and go for a couple of months. But the medics apparently did some remarkable ground-breaking treatment and rehab work. She eventually recovered, but she has lost her mobility and after many weeks of therapy, she was able to get back to work, but now in a wheelchair. I was only on the fringes of all this, of course, but my predecessor gave her a senior research job here where her years of experience with Tom really paid off. So now I think she has earned a promotion and a new start in this future development role, as I described to you just now".

"That's terrific, Alistair," said Bob. "Wish her luck from her pals at Langley and tell her we'll give any support she needs from over this side of the pond. In fact, you have just given me the idea that we really need to find the same degree of focus on new technologies here as well. At present, it is all happening in different sections of the agency, but you make me think that it is becoming so specialised and challenging now that we need to have some central coordination like you. Thanks so much for your time Alistair. Come and see us soon."

"You bet - and stay in touch," he replied.

CHAPTER EIGHT

The New Director's Office

The following Monday morning, "Trisha" Wells arrived at Thames House at 8am as usual and manoeuvred her wheelchair to the lift and up to the 3rd floor. As she arrived at the door of the Operations group she was met by Gordon Livesey, now the acting director:

"Good morning and congratulations," he said, giving her a hug. She responded warmly and realised that her colleague now knew about the change of job which the chief had described to her during the previous week. He continued: "Things have been busy here over the weekend and the offices next door have been improved quite a bit to welcome the new Director of Development. Come and see.".

They moved a few yards along the wide corridor and Trisha was amazed to see that new double doors had been fitted to the next office entrance and with a sign showing her name and new title. Then as she got closer in her wheelchair, she gasped as the new doors swung open automatically. Gordon followed her inside where she then saw that the executive-sized desk and other smart office furniture had all been arranged with space for her to move around easily. There was a conference table with six chairs and an adjoining door, also double size, which led to a larger office area with four desks ready for her new staff. Computers and phones were already installed, and Trisha could hardly believe what she was seeing.

"The downside of all this is that I shall miss you heading up the research team," said Gordon. "But this is a crucial new job and you will now be just next door to me ... with your crystal ball."

At that moment, Alistair McLaren, walked in from the lift, greeted them both, and asked: "How does this look to you, Trisha?"

She shook her head, disbelievingly. "This is amazing - your people here certainly moved fast to do all this over the weekend," she said. "But I guess I should not be surprised."

He suggested that she should try out her new desk and helped as she moved her wheelchair to a comfortable position. The two men then sat opposite her and as she relaxed in her new surroundings, Alistair told them:

"Okay, now you are my new top team – for the present and the future of the agency – and I know how well you two worked together to stay on top of everything after Tom retired. As you know, Gordon will only be here for a year or two until he takes a well-earned retirement. But his experience is going to be so important in the months ahead until we have found a new and long-term permanent successor in that crucial job."

"I'll do my best, sir," replied Gordon. "But I shall miss Patricia's input – or do I gather that we now say Trisha? She has been terrific since she came back full-time and she is right up to date on the new technology area so this new job is spot on. I can assure you that we will work well together when we need to."

"I am sure you will," replied the DG. "And I have some more news for Trisha. I have arranged for two bright young researchers from GCHQ to come to London to join your team for the time being. This will give you some resources to get the work of your new section started. If you get together with Emily from Human Resources, she will give you their details. They are due to report here in the next week or two and you will see that they are both well experienced in the new technology areas. Also, your start-up budget will enable you to engage a couple of research assistants right away. And when you are ready, I shall be looking for your organisation plans and budget requirements for the longer term. So good luck and remember my door is always open for you".

Then turning back as he left, he told them with a chuckle, "But it doesn't open automatically like your door here."

Gordon waited a few minutes while Trisha switched on the new computer on her desk and checked that the two phones were the same as those she was familiar with – one of them red for secure conversations. Then he asked, delicately: "By the way, where does Trisha come from?"

"It was the boss," she replied with a smile. "To be friendly, I think he wanted to call me Pat. But that has always been my brother Patrick, so he kind of settled on Trisha which is what some of my girl-friends use anyway, so I am used to it."

"Okay, and I can get used to it too," he replied and as he left, he told her: "I guess we both have work to do so good luck and let me know if I can help in any way. One of my girls can come in if you need anything – just buzz."

Trisha looked around her smart new surroundings, appreciating the view of the River Thames in the morning sunshine as well as the freshly decorated office and elegant new furnishings. Then she decided that job one was to talk to Human Resources – but first there was a visit to the adjoining rest room where she was amazed again to discover the door opening automatically as she approached!

Then, trying to relax at her big desk, she used her new internal phone for the first time to call Emily, who said she had been expecting the call and would be there to see her in a few minutes.

Emily Pearson was an elegant and confident executive, looking younger than her 49 years. She had been the senior manager in the HR department at MI5 for the past six years, after moving from a similar position in the Home Office. She greeted Trisha with congratulations on her appointment as a Director and added: "Since this is a new position which Alistair has created, I guess there are no terms of reference or even a job description yet – but that can wait".

"Yes, I will work on those with you as soon as possible," replied Trisha. "What else do I need to do?"

Emily continued: "The most important thing is to look at these files of the two researchers coming here from GCHQ in Cheltenham on temporary assignments. Alistair chose them to help you get things started. Their records look pretty impressive and they seem to confirm that GCHQ gets the pick of the graduates these days. I will leave these details with you to study as well as the details on four applicants we have identified here to consider as your research assistants."

She handed over two slim folders each marked Strictly Confidential – one with the name of Viraj Gupta and the other was Tina Heathcott. After quietly noting these interesting names of the DG's choices for her department, Trisha put them aside for later and moved on to discuss the potential research assistants for the new section. Emily described them as three strong internal applicants who were looking for promotion to the higher grade as assistant to a senior manager, plus one strong external candidate who was already known to them and had already been through the security check for the agency. "I will leave all these files with you to browse through in your own time," she said. "And we can have another meeting in a day or two to get your reactions. Meanwhile, I understand that Gordon next door will share one of his staff for anything you need."

"Ah yes," said Trisha. "That is very thoughtful of him. So let's start with a cup of coffee and a chat if you can spare the time?" With that, Emily went to the next office to request two coffees and the two women spent the next half hour catching up on their respective lives and careers .....

CHAPTER NINE

The Kremlin Test

In Moscow, the second test of the new laser device was taking place in the Kremlin. A group of four senior security executives were gathered in the 'protected' conference room and were briefed by Yuri Bortsov about the plan. He explained how Vasiliev, one of the research technicians, was outside with a security escort and the new secret listening system the technical team had developed.

"We will just sit around the table here chatting as usual and I will stay in contact with Vasiliev," he told them.

After a few minutes, Bortsov used his mobile phone to reach Vasiliev and asked where he was located. The group heard his reply: "I am outside the block where you are now, by the main entrance. And I am just tuning in to hear your voice when you put the phone down. Call me back in a few minutes and I will give you an update."

The group decided to chat about unimportant matters like the weather, their vacation plans and the football results until Bortsov thought it was time to check on progress. Vasiliev came on to the mobile phone again and told the group: "You got the score wrong – Dynamo beat Spartak 4-1 last night and not 3-1. I could hear your voices quite clearly."

As they all looked at each other with disbelief, Bortsov told the technician to move further away to another location with one further block of the building between them and then carry out a further test. After that, he should ask the security guard to bring him up to the conference room where they had assembled – and to bring the equipment with him.

While they waited, they discussed how the sound-proofing of the conference room had clearly been penetrated and what improvements could be made. "Of course, it is early days but there are many possibilities for using this invention around the world," said Bortsov. "But we also need to know whether a similar system might also be developed by other countries?"

Vasiliev and his escort eventually arrived, set up his equipment and began by showing the group of senior officials the small device which was used remotely to transmit and receive the laser signals. He then explained the small unit which could then receive the information and convert it into a voice recorder.

"This is an even smaller receiver than the one we demonstrated to you last week," explained the researcher. "So we have not yet perfected the link to a speaker system, but if I pass around my headset, you will all be able to hear your voices which were received in both locations outside."

One at a time, the group listened quietly to the conversations they had shared earlier. "It is clear, but very faint," said one of them and Vasiliev explained that he had expected the quality to be affected by the sound proofing of the room, but that this was an important test for his system which was still in the development phase."

The discussion went on for 30 minutes with more technical questions but overall it was agreed that this was a very significant piece of work and that the technical team should be congratulated. Bortsov added that he was already planning another test when the time was right - this time in an overseas location – but that meanwhile, it was top secret.

He did not suspect that at that moment, there was another urgent exchange of top security calls between MI5 in London and the CIA in the USA.

"According to GCHQ, the satellites have picked up another laser transmission in Moscow," Sir Alistair told Bob Smithers, who was able to respond by saying that the American monitoring agency had now reported the same new and mysterious development in the past hour.

"Our guys are still analysing the information and we will keep you in the picture," said the CIA chief. "But we are thinking of following up by getting one of our Moscow informants to nose around. We have one sleeper there who is a great guy – he works for the Moscow refuse collection department so he can move around the city pretty well. He stays well clear of the American embassy for obvious reasons and has set up a communication chain which comes to us via our embassy team in Vienna. What do you think?"

"You obviously trust your source, Bob, so it won't do any harm and meanwhile, we will also keep our Moscow eyes and ears open," replied Sir Alistair. He then added: "By the way, we also have our researchers at GCHQ studying the signals and trying to work out the possible applications of laser technology."

They agreed to keep information on this subject top secret at this stage and liaise on the red phones when necessary. But the MI5 chief in

London decided to also brief the experienced head of the agency's Russia and Eastern Europe section, Oliver Brown, and also his acting Director of Operations, Gordon Livesey.

They were soon in his office, where he described the mysterious signals picked up by observation satellites over Moscow and added: "Just see if your informants know about anything going on at the Kremlin around the times that these signals have been picked up? Don't get any wires crossed with our friends in Langley just yet. And don't mention the use of lasers to anyone at this stage".

CHAPTER TEN

The New Team

Trisha moved slowly around her new office, with its smart furnishings and bookcases, with the growing feeling that she was going to enjoy working there on her new challenge. Then back at her empty desk, she called Gordon in the adjoining office and followed up his offer to loan one of his assistants to help her to settle in.

"Sure thing – I will send Jane in right away," he said. "And let me know if there is any way I can help, preferably this afternoon when my diary is clear."

Jane was a smartly suited senior secretary with nearly 15 years experience at the agency. To start the process, the two women went to the floor below and the office used by Trisha for the six months since her return to work in the Operations section. Together, they packed the files and documents from the desk and its drawers into cardboard boxes, then the books from her shelves, and finally the precious photographs and souvenirs which were on the desktop. Then there were two family photographs and a colourful oriental picture which hung on the wall.

Helped by two young men she quickly recruited from elsewhere in the department, they loaded it all on a small trolley and wheeled it via the lift to the Director's floor above. Then Jane set about making her new office "look like home" - as she put it to a grateful and admiring Trisha.

When the job was done, she turned to the six personnel files which had been left with Trisha earlier. "I must get to work and go through these folders – they are the applications for the first new positions in my section," she said to Jane. "And for starters, I just hope that I can find someone as efficient and well-organised as you - so thanks for so much help. I will certainly give you a call if I need anything else."

Trisha started to study the four slim folders containing the applications and details of the applicants for the two positions as Research Assistants.

The first one was from Marion Vickery, who had a ten years background history at MI5 as a secretary in three different sections. She was now 48 and her experience was impressive. She came with excellent annual reports for her secretarial skills and Trisha knew her by sight as a smart and confident lady, well respected across the agency. Interesting, she thought – she will know where all the bodies are buried, but why had she not been promoted earlier in her career? Also, her previous applications for promotion – including one to switch her career and to become an analyst - had been unsuccessful.

Moving on, the next file was on Victoria Browning, another current member of the MI5 staff, a secretary in the finance department who she did not know. After graduating at Southampton University, she had trained at a secretarial college before applying to become a civil servant and joining as a secretary in the Cabinet Office. From there, she had moved to MI5 two years previously at a higher grade to become secretary to the agency's Finance Director. There were no negative comments in her file and at 27 she was clearly ambitious and had submitted a strong application for the position in the new Development directorate. This certainly impressed Trisha.

The third folder opened by Trisha was an application from a 26-years-old history graduate, Anthony Scott, who began his civil service career as a research assistant at the Home Office. His reports were impressive and he had recently applied for a move to MI5 as an analyst and in his application, he stressed his computer and technical expertise and his ambition to make his future in the security service. He was currently on a temporary attachment at Thames House in the archive section.

The fourth file was the only external candidate shortlisted for this new position. Charlotte Robbins was 32 and currently working with a public relations company specialising in the technology market. She had been recommended by an influential Member of Parliament who was impressed by her presentation at a conference on national security. She had claimed to have some knowledge of MI5 activities and had told him afterwards that she wanted to become part of it. Her application had already been reviewed by the Civil Service recruitment section and after a preliminary interview, it was then passed on to MI5 Human Resources.

Trisha began the process of narrowing it down to just two, and much as she was attracted by the approach of the fourth applicant, she knew that the Civil Service recruitment process would take time to complete, whereas the other three were already approved in that respect. She also recognised that the first one on her list was experienced and reliable, but also older than herself. She really wanted a young, enthusiastic team around her to confront all the new technologies they would be dealing with – and so she felt ready to discuss these applicants with the HR director.

Next, she turned to the two larger folders on the two researchers selected by the DG for a temporary transfer from GCHQ to MI5, Viraj Gupta and Tina Heathcott. She knew these were *fait accompli*, at least for the time being – but she also knew that they could not have had a better recommendation than being chosen by Sir Alistair himself.

She was impressed to read that Gupta was just 27 and regarded as a high-flyer when he graduated from Cambridge with a "First" in science and astro-physics. He had been educated in the UK when his father was a diplomat at the Indian embassy in London and had impressed the Civil Service recruiters who interviewed students after their final university year. This led to his career starting as a research assistant at the Home Office. Eager to move on, he had applied for a job as an analyst at GCHQ which required computer and technical expertise. His work there earned him a position with the technical staff of the agency where he went on to carry out some special assignments from the Deputy Director, Alistair McLaren, no less.

"I look forward to meeting him" thought Trisha as she turned her attention to Tina Heathcott. The name rang a bell – so she quickly Googled her name and discovered that one of her family had been a leading Conservative politician who served as Chancellor of the Exchequer in the Government in the 1950's. Another had been an MP. So it was not surprising to also discover that after earning a degree in Life Sciences at Oxford University, she had started work at the Conservative party headquarters. Next, she moved on to become a researcher for a Member of Parliament at the House of Commons, before applying to join the Civil Service and securing a research position at GCHQ. She was now 31 and reports in the file described how her past experiences and strong work ethic had obviously impressed the top management at the agency, including Sir Alistair of course.

And so Trisha had almost made up her mind about the start-up team to support her in her new role. She was confident about the two very different personalities chosen as her two researchers from GCHQ and looked forward to meeting them both. So she called the Human Resources office to arrange another meeting with Emily as soon as possible to discuss the six personnel files they had provided

CHAPTER ELEVEN

Target London

Yuri Bortsov followed the tradition for strong and dominant heads of Russia's secret service, the FSB directorate. His style was to celebrate the agency's successes, to reward positive results and to ignore failures – "which never happened". One of his most experienced operators, Yakov Razovsky was currently on a razor's edge for his career prospects. He had been highly regarded as head of the secret service's bureau at the London embassy until he made a major error during the mission by the infamous "Russian Lieutenant". This had resulted in him facing an embarrassing high publicity court case as an accomplice in the death of a British naval employee and he was sentenced to eight years in jail.

It was the tradition of the agency to celebrate it's successes, to reward positive results and to ignore failures l- like two missing agents "which never happened".

The chief now had a new plan and decided to call again on Razovsky, who had done an impressive job on updating their files on the new team at the UK's secret services. But it was still with some apprehension that he answered the call to join a meeting upstairs with the director and three of his senior staff.

Bortsov gave him a somewhat gruff welcome, and then surprised him by saying: "Sit down, Yazov. I want your ideas about an important and highly secret London operation I am planning. You know the territory there better than anyone else here, so I want to describe it to you."

He went on to outline the system devised by their in-house technical development team to penetrate secret meeting rooms by means of a laser beam which enabled discussions to be overheard and recorded. He then described the two tests they had carried out in the previous days, one from outside his own office building and then one at the Kremlin where a supposedly high security conference room is located.

"What is more," he continued. "The equipment is quite small and portable and appears to be operational from two blocks distance from the target. So I want to find a way to eventually equip all our major overseas units with one of these systems. It could then get us one step ahead of the plans our adversaries are making. How does that sound to you? The question is this – how would it work in London and even in Washington?"

Razovsky had listened intently and was flattered to be asked for his advice on such an important development. "This sounds really interesting and I can think of two locations in London which might be vulnerable" he replied. And then, after a moment of thought, he asked: "But what is the actual range of the system? How close does the equipment need to be in order to receive a signal?"

The chief replied that this was a crucial question and said the technicians were still working on refinements for the system, which was quite new. He explained that the most important piece of the equipment was a small disc – "about the size of a saucer" – which could be easily concealed close to the target building. This unit then re-transmitted the signal to the recording device located further away but the actual range, he added, was still the subject of the tests being made.

"There are certainly nearby hotels which could be used as listening points near two government departments I can think of - and with some further research, we can probably find several more good targets."," suggested Razovsky. Then he added: "But of course, this area of London is closely guarded by patrolling security police and they would quickly spot anything new and would move any parked vehicles".

"Yes of course, and I really want you to go to London to do some discrete tests," said Bortsov. "You know your way around and had some good contacts there, so you are just the man to do this. But I think you are still blacklisted for a diplomatic visa after your experience in their jails. So unless you can think of a way to get round this, how about directing the operation from here if you had the right agent in London to work with you at long range?"

"Let me think about it," came the thoughtful reply. "It could probably work, but it is now 3 years since I was operating there and things change quickly. Government offices are moved, security systems are updated, and so on. Could we also think about ways to get me there as a tourist via a third country, say via Spain or Ireland? Come to think about it, maybe Madrid or Dublin might be softer targets?"

Bortsov paused and considered this suggestion, and Razovsky added: "If I go, I don't think I should be carrying this test equipment in my luggage."

This brought a rare laugh from the group who began to relax as the FSB chief went on to describe how his plan also included sending one of their key technicians to the London embassy, posing as the regular courier and concealing the equipment in a diplomatic bag.

The others looked alarmed by this suggestion and the chief sought to reassure them.

"I have checked the rules and they are pretty loose - and there is no definition of how big or small the bag must be," he said. And then, quoting from his notes, he continued: "This is what the book says - a diplomatic bag usually has some form of lock and/or tamper-evident seal attached to it to deter or detect interference by unauthorized third parties. As long as it is externally marked to show its status, the bag has diplomatic immunity from search or seizure".[

With that, he rounded off the discussion, telling his now-relaxing colleague: "I know this would be a bit risky, so we need more ideas in the next few days. But keep it to yourselves and think it through. But I believe that this project could be a game-changer if we can get it right".

CHAPTER TWELVE

Ilia's New Challenge

Later that day, it was the turn of the young agent Pavlov Ilia who was surprised to be called to the top floor for a private meeting with the Yuri Bortsov. Widely believed to be man destined succeed as President at some time in the future, Bortsov was ruthless and dominant. He could be overbearing with his own senior staff - and had a reputation for extravagant celebrations of his division's successes while ignoring and then demoting any of his team involved in mistakes or failures.

From the most recent intake of young operators and agents from the FSB's training academy, he had been impressed by the demeanour of the 30-years-old recruit. His documents showed that he graduated in international affairs, had good foreign language skills and he showed a quietly determined attitude - "a bit like me at that age," Bortsov confided to one of his top deputies.

After a short spell in the research section, Ilia was soon promoted to be the youngest agent in the agency. He became friendly with another new agent, Nikolai Aldanov, who was 12 years older, having already served as an officer in the

Russian navy He had risen to the rank of Lieutenant before taking an opportunity to leave the service to start a second career with Russia's foreign intelligence agency, the FSB in Moscow. But he remained as an officer in the navy reserve with annual training commitments.

While working in the research section, Aldanov had been eager to make his name as an agent in the field and to get overseas assignments. Among other creative projects, he decided to try on-line dating and he placed his own photograph, in smart naval uniform, on an international website. His idea seemed to have paid off when he had a response from a woman in England who worked for the Royal Navy at the dockyard in Portsmouth. In the exchanges which followed, he discovered that the navy was not their only common interest but that her family had emigrated from Russia in the 1930s and she was interested to discover more about her ancestors.

Aldanov persuaded his chief that this link to someone in one of Britain's major naval bases was too good an opportunity to miss. They evolved a plan whereby he would 'rejoin' the navy and get a posting on a Russian ship due to visit Portsmouth for refuelling during a future training voyage in the Atlantic. The couple eventually met but in their first evening together in Portsmouth, the woman's apartment was raided by the British police and security services. The couple's careless on-line messages had been intercepted by MI5!

Aldanov was arrested and charged with espionage - and was still held in a high security prison awaiting trial when he was unexpectedly returned to Russia in a spy-swap, which happened to be convenient for both countries.

He remained in limbo for several months and could not return to work for the FSB - but he was eventually re-employed by the government in the foreign affairs ministry and assigned to a minor role as naval attache at the Russian embassy in Japan. Other than routine reports, there was little for him to do - until he became a victim in a shooting incident in a Tokyo karaoke bar which he was visiting with a colleague from the embassy. Aldanov suffered an arm wound but was relatively unscathed. However, the event made big news and he became another embarrassment to his chiefs in Moscow - as had his previous episode in Portsmouth.

This was when Bortsov had first turned to Ilia: "You know Aldanov", he said, and went on to describe the latest story from Japan. He continued: "So I want you to go to Tokyo at once and work with our Ambassador there to track him down, sort it out and bring him back."

Ilia flew to Japan the next day and succeeded in making contact with Aldanov at the courtroom where he was appearing as a key witness at the trial of two Japanese gunmen. They had a positive meeting, but the next day Aldanov was 'snatched' in a smart move by agents from America's CIA, who then flew him to the USA and persuaded him to not only defect, but to work with the agency. And so Bortsov turned to Ilia once more - "Go and find him again and this time, do the necessary - he is a traitor!"

Aldanov was located by Ilia, who discovered him living in an apartment convenient to the American agency HQ. Working with the locally-based FSB agents, they decided to hire a local expert gunman from the criminal fraternity in Washington and together, they tracked the traitor and killed him with one gunshot while he was out jogging early one morning.

Now, months later, at Ilia's private meeting with Bortsov, the FSB chief explained that he wanted a repeat success - but this time in London, together with one of their technology experts.

"I want you to travel there with Vasiliev who is going there soon to test a new technical spying system. And while you are there, our locally-based agents will find a suitable location for the test to take place. They are searching to discover a location where an important meeting takes place, hopefully including one or two of top British government people. I want you to find a way to get one of them - I don't mind who."

He added that he had briefed the chief of the FSB unit in London to issue whatever equipment Ilia needed from their secret armoury. The young agent was thoughtful for a few moments, then said he appreciated being chosen for this assignment and looked forward to his first visit to London. And so Birtsov concluded the meeting: "I will leave it to you, Ilia. So good luck".

"Thank you. I understand, sir," said a still perplexed Ilia as he stood up and left the room - thinking "Why me?"

CHAPTER THIRTEEN

Dinner at The Club

Sir Alistair had now hit the ground running in his new role, with his 'action now' in-box full of current threats to the UK's security. These included the discovery of a possible new spy network being created in the North of England with Russian connections as well as a covert Moslem group planning to disrupt future events with royal family involvement. Then there was a new report on a growing number of illegal immigrants arriving in the UK with records of violence and criminality. And this led to concerns in Parliament over the delays in deporting convicted foreign nationals.

There was also a preliminary report prepared by Gordon Livesey following up on the murder of Tom Stacey and his wife. It listed all the contacts Tom had made during the past year and it went on to set out a range of possible anti-Russia reprisals. The Operations division was clearly being pro-active in the way the new DG expected and he focussed first on reading Livesey's detailed analysis. He soon decided that since the origins of this crucial matter predated his arrival at MI5, it would be useful to discuss it with his experienced predecessor. So he called Sir Charles Bentley who was happy to arrange a quiet dinner at his London club that evening, and he welcomed the suggestion that they should include Gordon Livesey.

The drive to The Mall in the DG's chauffer driven car was a new experience for Gordon. So too was the grandeur of the club, where his former boss was waiting to welcome them and escort them to the elegant dining room. "Your usual table, Sir Charles?" asked the head waiter as he escorted them to a quiet corner table. The introductory small talk soon turned to business over a glass of dry sherry and Gordon relaxed as the DG explained the current focus on following up the tragic deaths of Tom Spencer and his wife. And he congratulated Gordon on his initial report on reprisals targeting Russia which had triggered the dinner meeting.

Sir Charles said he understood and went on to recall that during his years at MI5 there had been several previous events which had led to a reprisal being secretly organised. He described one which had focussed on targeting the enormous investments of Russian oligarchs living in the West as a way of putting indirect pressure on the Kremlin leadership. "This is an on-going operation of course", he added. "With the cooperation of some international banking experts."

The DG said he had been studying this programme as well as confidential reports of how they had quietly 'taken out' known Russian agents in other countries – which brought a wry smile from Gordon, who had been involved in some of these secret operations.

The veteran MI6 man then recalled that a few months earlier, there had been the Russian drone raid on the home of the American Ambassador in London. "They responded to that very quickly by shipping half a dozen diplomats from the Washington embassy back to Moscow", he added. "And because of the strong links that Tom had created with the CIA, we might get them to work with us on a joint UK and US operation – perhaps a squeeze on those oligarch assets. That would really hurt."

Sir Alistair listened intently and added: "From what I have seen, this raid on Russian finances becomes a very complex business. And it seems to take a long time because of all the legal complications, but the operation certainly gets the attention of the plutocrats. What else did you find in Tom's secret files, Gordon?"

"Well, he had a pretty comprehensive assessment of all the key people at the FSB headquarters in Moscow as well as their agents based in overseas embassies," he replied. "And he obviously had a way to track their movements, but I have not yet worked out all his sources of information - I am sure there is much more locked away somewhere?"

"Have you talked to Patricia Wells about this yet?" asked Sir Charles. "She worked very closely with Tom as his assistant for several years and probably knows more about his activities than anyone else here?"

"Good idea," replied Gordon. "I will do that tomorrow if you agree, Alistair, and I will let you know. I guess she will also understand why Tom had a grudging respect for the FSB boss called Bortsov. There was one very comprehensive file on him which assessed his strengths and weaknesses – all very interesting".

"What weaknesses?" asked the DG.

"I need to read more," said Gordon. "On the one hand he was very arrogant and was obviously not popular with his senior staff. At the same time, he had a soft spot for his family, especially two teenage sons who he was encouraging to follow in his footsteps and sometimes took to meetings with him".

"Aha," said Alistair, thoughtfully. "That could be a real weakness to exploit, Gordon. Can you work on the information sources to discover more about those sons, where they live, where they go, who they know, and so on?"

As the dinner progressed, another suggestion from the retired DG was to research the current Russian activities in Africa. He went on to list the territories he thought might be vulnerable – such as Mali, Niger, Chad and the Central African Republic. "We know there is the build-up of mercenaries there, as well as investments in mineral resources and an expanding number of experts – or maybe spies? - now based in their embassies. Actually, this is one of the areas we assigned Patricia Wells to research a few months ago, working together with the African desk at MI6. Maybe you can find out how that is going?"

The trio mulled over various aspects of these ideas and how each of them could be implemented, They also enjoyed a leisurely dinner, shared a bottle of Burgundy followed by coffee and cognac – and finally agreed that this had been a productive dinner. And it was also a meeting that had never happened!

CHAPTER FOURTEEN

The Team Takes Shape

At Thames House, Trisha Wells had an early visit from Gordon Livesey who asked her to prepare a confidential memorandum on Tom Spencer's assessment of Yuri Bortsov, including his vulnerabilities, (if any?). She was eager to help, recalling that when they worked together, she had learned a great deal about his views on the top individuals in Russian hierarchy – "some of it were his personal views which did not figure in his official reports," she added, cautiously.

These recollections began to come to mind during the day as she set about the task of reorganising her filing system and books, with the help of Jane from the next office. She also took a call from Emily Pearson in Human Resources to ask if she would be available the following afternoon?

"The DG has arranged for his two people from GCHQ to be in London for the day tomorrow and he thought you might like to look them over?" said Emily. "As you know by now, their names are Viraj Gupta and Tina Heathcott and I expect you have had a good look at their files?"

"Yes, and I am impressed by what I have read," said Trisha, beginning to feel more confident about her new challenge. "That sounds like a really good idea. Do you think I should see them separately or together?"

"Together, I would suggest," replied Emily. "It is not a job interview because they have already been assigned to join your department by Alistair so I suggest that it would be better to start creating a team approach. It has all been arranged as a temporary transfer for three months to get you started and if it is okay with you, Alistair says he will bring them into your office at about two pm to make the introductions and I think he then plans to leave you to it."

Trisha said this sounded like a good idea, and then Emily went on to suggest another meeting in the morning to review the four applications for the assistant positions in the new division and they settled on 9am. And so – in addition to making notes about the Russians to share with Gordon – she also reviewed the personnel files again to prepare for the next day, and prepared draft job descriptions for her two assistants. She had already reached some preliminary preferences, but as she took the four files from her desk drawer again, it was time for her to make her first executive decisions as the new Director of Future Development.

And so, the next morning, she was ready for an early meeting with the HR Director. "So what do you think of them?" asked Emily Pearson.

"On the basis of these files," said Trisha, "I would go with Anthony Scott and Victoria Browning – but I also like the look of the external candidate, Charlotte Robbins. When can I have an interview with them?"

"You can talk to the first two of them today if you like?" replied Emily. "And of course, they could be available to start as soon as their current jobs here can be covered. I agree that Charlotte is an impressive candidate too. She interviewed well when we had a preliminary session a couple of weeks ago and is very confident and ambitious, so I can easily get her to come back again?"

"OK - then let's do that," said Trisha, decisively. "Can you get those two internal people to come to meet me today - maybe after I have seen the couple from GCHQ this afternoon? Can we also talk more about Charlotte's availability before I make a final decision? I want to get things moving as soon as possible and as you will see from the job descriptions I prepared, these two posts will be mainly providing back-up support for the two people coming from GCHQ".

She handed her proposed new job descriptions to the HR Director and added: "And by the way, I don't think I should continue to share Jane from Gordon's office next door once we get going, so is there any way I can have my own secretary or PA?"

"If the DG agrees, that should be no problem," said Emily, as she left to return to her own office to follow up the discussion. Meanwhile, Trisha was also thinking about the afternoon meeting with the DG and his two chosen operators from GCHQ when Emily called with news: "As I hoped, Anthony and Victoria are both in the office today and could easily spare half an hour this morning if that works for you?"

Trisha replied eagerly: "Why not!" and within 10 minutes, Anthony arrived at her office. He paused as he entered the impressive and spacious new executive office and quickly apologised for his tee shirt, jeans and sneakers – "We are a bit casual down in the library," he explained. She quickly put him at his ease and was impressed by his confidence and demeanour as she invited him to sit by her desk. She explained how her new department was tasked with researching new technologies which could affect the way MI5 operated in the next decade and that the two positions of research assistant would provide support for two experienced operators who would be joining her on loan from GCHQ.

"That sounds right up my street," said an excited Anthony. "This is exactly the area I wanted to work on when I applied to join MI5". As he went on and asked some pertinent questions, Trisha could not fail to be impressed.

Next came Victoria Browning, business-like and smart, as rather expected from the Finance division. She focussed closely on the outline of the new department's challenge and then told Trisha: "From where I am now, I get an overview of all the exciting activities the agency is working on but this sounds like a real opportunity to move on in a new direction. And I am really excited by all the new technology areas in my career so far."

It was a productive hour for Trisha, and after further thought, she decided to wait until the afternoon session with the two researchers from GCHQ before sharing her decision with Emily.

CHAPTER FIFTEEN

The Bag Arrives

The daily Aeroflot flight from Moscow landed on time at London's Heathrow airport. As usual, the manifest, showing the names of the aircrew and all passengers had been notified in advance to the UK Immigration authorities, who routinely shared the details with MI5.

The information was reviewed by the surveillance team in the National Security section while the flight was still en route. They focussed interest on the two names listed by the Russian foreign ministry as new appointees to the London embassy – Pavlov Ilia, was listed as diplomatic courier and Igor Vasiliev was described as technical assistant. There was a parallel memorandum from the Russian embassy to the UK Foreign Office advising the names of the two members of the current staff who would be returning to Moscow, thus retaining the mutually agreed staffing levels.

It was assumed that Ilia, as the nominated courier, would be bringing the usual diplomatic bag to be taken to the Russian Embassy in Kensington Palace Gardens. And that Vasiliev, a new name to the MI5 surveillance team, would be replacing one of the current group of telecoms experts at the embassy.

Then, making some further research, it was found that Ilea had last been listed in UK intelligence files as an agent based at the Russian embassy in Washington DC in the last year. The records also described him as: "A suspect involved in the shooting of the former Russian agent Aldanov, who had defected to work for the CIA". A quick check with contacts at CIA confirmed that Ilia had recently been replaced in the Washington DC embassy lists and was shown as returning to Moscow.

When this information appeared on Gordon Livesey's screen, he passed an instruction to the team at the airport to "keep a close eye on these two."

As usual, the two Russians were greeted on board the aircraft by a Foreign Office official and a Special Branch police officer, and they disembarked from the aircraft first. They were escorted through the VIP arrivals area to an immigration desk where the official checked their paperwork and visas before they moved on to collect baggage. The customs check found nothing abnormal and according to international tradition, the locked leather case carried by Ilia carried the correct identification as the diplomatic bag and was not inspected. And so, less than 20 minutes after landing, the new arrivals were on their way into the capital in a Russian embassy limousine.

They were unaware that while they had been waiting in the customs area, the padlocked travel case identified as the diplomatic bag had been discretely scanned by the head of the security operation – revealing more than just paperwork. He could identify a wrapped object which appeared on his discrete screens to be a small radio or mobile phone. He made an urgent call from the airport to the MI5 headquarters where Gordon Livesey advised him not to interfere with the arrivals' baggage. "We will check out your scans more carefully as soon as we can," he was told. "And meanwhile, we will be making sure that Special Branch keeps a close tab on the movements of these two individuals."

In less than an hour, there was a confidential report on the monitor screens of both the DG and Operations Director at MI5 about the new arrivals from Moscow which described how the secret scans had shown that the diplomatic bag actually contained two small items of technical equipment; also that at least one of the individuals appeared to have cables and small switches hidden in the lining of his clothing.

When the DG reviewed the report, he immediately called his operations director and asked: "So what do you make of that?"

"We can certainly take action about the mis-use of the diplomatic bag later," came the brisk reply from Gordon Livesey. "And our technical people are already taking a more careful look at those scans to see what to make of them. I think we will discover more by putting extra surveillance at the Russian embassy and a tail on both those new arrivals for the next week or two and to follow them wherever they go. We will also set up enhanced monitoring of any signals in and out of the embassy".

"Right - that's a plan – let me know any developments", concluded the chief.

CHAPTER SIXTEEN

"He Did What?

As the official limousine from Heathrow airport approached the elegant Russian embassy in London's fashionable Kensington Palace Gardens, the first thing that Pavlov Ilia and Igor Vasiliev noticed were the two prominent blue and yellow striped police cars parked nearby. The iron gates swung open automatically and they were soon inside to be welcomed by FSB's station chief, Ivan Lebedev. The two Russian travellers were making their first visit to Britain and as they were led to the chief's office, they carefully carried the diplomatic bag and the other small items of equipment they had smuggled into the country. Waiting for them in the office were two more members of the staff based at the embassy, introduced by Lebedev as their technology experts.

After a few words of welcome and introduction, the chief said he had been briefed by his boss in Moscow, Yuri Bortsov, and he knew that this was a highly important and secret mission. "So what do you have here to show us?" he asked.

Vasiliev then explained that with his team in Moscow, they had developed a system which used laser-type transmissions which could penetrate walls and feed back signals which were then be converted into voice format. This technology, he said, had the potential to enable secret conversations to be heard inside a remote location with a direct line of sight to the target.

"Our first demonstrations at our headquarters and then in the Kremlin were successful," he continued. "And we have now developed this smaller and more portable version which Mr. Bortsov wanted us to test in an overseas location – and especially to see if it could be concealed through airport checks. And so far, so good."

"Maybe you were just lucky," commented the more cautious Lebedev, with his greater experience of international travel. "Anyway, you are here so show us how it works?"

Vasiliev then prepared their demonstration, as they had practised in Moscow, with Ilia taking the small unit into the next room, together with one of the two embassy technicians, and closing the door behind him. The others continued their conversation for about 2 minutes – and then Ilia returned and was able to demonstrate a replay of their discussion about the London weather. He then showed them the small microphone and explained how it could be located separately and even concealed.

"Okay, that's a good start," commented Lebedev. "But you said the range can be from further away and even through more than one wall. This is a pretty solid old building and there is a courtyard outside at the rear, so do you think you can do the same from there?"

Ilia understood the challenge and was taken through two doors and a corridor to reach the open area, taking care to note the direction of the office where they had been meeting. He then helped Vasiliev to set up the miniature transmitter unit on a wall and went a further 20 yards away with the laser unit. Within a minute of searching, he was able to locate and hear the conversation they had left behind. When they returned to the office, they impressed their colleagues by replaying the conversation as clearly as in the previous recording.

Lebedev asked a few searching questions and it was explained that this new technology of microwave-laser transmission had been developed by his team in Moscow to carry and then play back voice signals. The two technicians also had questions about a technological development which was new to them. We know about lasers," they said. "But this is something else!"

Lebedev was clearly impressed and he decided to call the Russian Ambassador and invite him to come down from his second floor office to see a demonstration. After a brief introduction and description of the system, Vasiliev and Ilia did it all again and the Ambassador nodded approvingly and said he could recognise the potential uses to penetrate almost any confidential meeting. "Yes", replied Vasiliev. "Even in rooms which have been sound-proofed, which we demonstrated to the top people at the Kremlin".

"So where do we go from here?" asked Ambassador Andreev. "This seems to be an amazing new development and thank you for bringing it here. I now understand why Bortsov said he wanted us to find a location here in London to demonstrate the way in which this could be deployed anywhere in the world. It could change everything."

Then he paused, thoughtfully, and asked Vasiliev: "How did you bring this equipment into the country?"

"Oh, Ilia brought most of it in the diplomatic bag," replied the technician, naively, only for the Ambassador to explode – **"He did what?"**

After a deep breath or two, he continued: "Well, don't ever mention that again, to anybody. Okay? That was a huge risk and I will take it up confidentially with Moscow. Maybe you got away with it? But I would not be too sure – anyway, let's get on with it."

It was agreed that Vasiliev and Ilia would work with the technical experts at the Embassy to set up a more realistic test. One of the most experienced agents based at the embassy would then work with them to find their way around the city to decide on a suitable test location. The group began to study maps and photographs, and Andreev suggested that rather than risk working in the well-guarded government office area of Westminster, they should carry out research to find out where a private meeting would be taking place elsewhere in London – and hopefully one which would be attended by at least one senior government officer.

He added: "Actually, one of my special assistants has been here for years and she knows everything that goes on in London. I don't know much about her sources, but she has a network which always comes up with an answer. So I will brief her about this requirement and I am sure she will come up with something pretty soon and I will let you know."

Meanwhile, it was decided that the two men from Moscow would be taken on a familiarisation tour, after settling into a nearby hotel used regularly by visitors to the embassy.

CHAPTER SEVENTEEN

Concepts From GCHQ

It was an important day for Trisha Wells at Thames House. She was now ready to put together her team and start the work which her new directorate had been established to perform. She began by meeting the agency's Human Resources Director, Emily Pearson again, to share her thoughts after studying once more the six personnel files about her potential team.

"I am so impressed by the quality and enthusiasm of all these people," she began. "And I am looking forward to meeting the two from GCHQ this afternoon. In their new roles here, I am expecting them to be out and about most of the time, researching new developments and getting input from the best brains in the business about what to expect in years to come"

She then turned to the support staff and said she hoped the two research assistants she had chosen would be a couple of worker bees. Their job was to do the follow up work, maintain the records and produce the analysis of new technology which the agency can use for its future planning.

"So Emily, my suggestion is this," she continued. I would like to offer the two jobs to Anthony Scott and Charlotte Robbins. They are both ambitious and pro-active, but I realise there may be some delay while Charlotte goes through the Civil Service recruitment routines".

"Yes, that makes sense," replied Emily. "But I think we can expedite the process with Charlotte and get her on board within a month. And I know that Anthony will be really excited to move up here from his research job downstairs at the earliest opportunity."

Trisha then added: "But that's not all. I also want to talk about Victoria Browning. I think she is just what I need as my PA. She knows where all the bodies are buried here and understands all the routines and systems of the agency in the Finance Department and beyond. This will help to keep me on the front foot with administrative matters. So could it be a promotion for her to work for me if the DG approves the new position?"

"Certainly, and I don't think he will need much persuasion," said Emily, with a knowing smile. "He just wants you to get to work on his pet theme of discovering what the future holds. Leave it to me! He will be here after lunch with his two boys from Cheltenham."

And promptly as arranged, Sir Alistair walked into Trisha's sparkling new office with Tina Heathcott and Viraj Gupta following him. He greeted her with a peck on the cheek and introduced the newcomers as they sat around the conference table - both looking relaxed and comfortable. The DG began by pointing to the spacious empty room next door and told them: "That is where you will be based and I suspect that in a few weeks it will be as busy as your department in Cheltenham".

"Yes, and I hope it will be soon – so welcome," said Trisha. "I know that you both have the experience to help this new division to get up and running as soon as possible"

And she was pleased when the DG then added: "That could be very soon. If you need it, we have some temporary living accommodation available nearby from next Monday and so it can be as soon as they sort out their personal lives."

And he added to Trisha: "You will soon discover why I selected these two to get you started. You know all about their backgrounds and you will soon discover that they are both hyperactive - maybe in different ways. We always knew where they were, bothering us with new ideas and suggestions. So stand by. I have to get to a ministerial meeting by three so it's over to you – and good luck."

With that, he left the three of them to relax and Trisha was immediately impressed by their calm and relaxed composure. Viraj was a small man, in a fashionable casual jacket and chinos, clearly articulate but with a slight Asian accent and focussed on everything around him. By contrast, Tina was taller than her colleague, appeared mature for her 26 years, and wearing in a smart blue business suit. She was clearly eager to make an impression as being sophisticated and worldly. After each had said how much they were looking forward to a new and exciting challenge, they listened intently as Trisha described how she saw the next phase in developing the new "group 34" project, as she called it, with the two of them based in the adjoining office, together with two research assistants.

"In a phrase, I am looking to you to start the process of discovering all the new technologies and systems, anywhere in the world, which could become a risk and endanger the security of the UK in the next decade, "she began. "Once you have settled in and made your plans, I do not expect to see you here very much. I want you to be free to use your contacts and security clearance to get access to technology companies, research organisations, university specialists, security experts and anywhere else the inquiries may lead. Feel free to travel overseas if it seems necessary, but check your plans with me first before you travel so that we can agree your budgets and advise our embassies if necessary. Is that all ok with you?"

"Yes, that all makes sense to me," responded the enthusiastic Viraj. And Tina said she agreed and added: "This will be quite a contrast - we were both rather deskbound at GCHQ but I can see exactly what you have in mind."

"That's good," continued the new Director. "Take your time and don't try to do everything at once. There is much more unknown activity going on which we need to discover and we will be growing the department with more researchers over the coming months. I will leave it to you to agree where you might work together or go it alone, whatever makes sense in the circumstances. Your two researchers will soon be here to look after the shop, including your travel arrangements with our in-house experts.

"I'm sure you don't need me to tell you how to organise your new filing systems and maintain all the confidential information you discover. But I will hope to see your reports and analysis from time to time which I can review and share with the DG as necessary. We can have regular update meetings when possible so that I can brief the boss before he has to report to the Prime Minister's COBRA committee meetings.

"But to repeat myself, the bottom line is not just to discover developments and new systems, but also to identify their possible dangers ranging from assassinations to political unrest and terrorism – and many things in between. This requires blue sky thinking and if what you find surprises even you, then you are on the right track. Does that make sense so far?"

They both showed their understanding of this introduction and it was Tina who quickly responded. "That's quite a menu, Miss Wells, but I can see where you are heading and why you think this section will soon need more people. I can't wait to get started."

"Me too", said Viraj even more enthusiastically, and then in more measured tones, he added: "I can now see why this section has a very different set of objectives to our group in Cheltenham. But when we were briefed by Mr. McLaren last week – actually I mean Sir Alistair of course – he authorised me to prepare a summary of some of the new ideas which we already had in our sights. This may help to give you, and us, a head start."

He handed over a sealed envelope, which Trisha Wells opened carefully and she quickly skimmed the two pages of information – headed "TOP SECRET" – and with a list of six paragraphs in bold type.

"That's typical of Alistair," she said, trying to avoid looking too startled by her first impressions of the material. "I will study this carefully over the next day or two and then discuss it, and a lot more, when you come to join me. When do you think this can be?"

"How about next week – maybe even Monday," replied Tina, glancing at the diary on her cell phone.

After further discussion with Trisha about their own domestic arrangements, the two newcomers began to feel at home and looked forward to their new challenges before heading excitedly to their train journey back to Cheltenham. And as soon as they had left, Trisha settled down to concentrate on the document they brought and its unexpected contents. It read:

WHAT NEXT??? Some new concepts ....

An AI tool which can break any password, potentially creating massive data breaches, making cyber attacks possible on public databases and institutions.

A technology enabling satellites in orbit around the globe to be hacked by a rogue organisation, potentially stymying their operations and then demanding ransoms.

An AI technology which can painlessly decode brainwaves and then display thoughts of a user, which could be used in interrogations and thus threaten security.

A new laser technology that can record conversations inside a building via micro-seismic vibrations. These microwave lasers can detect the movement of air particles - even through walls – and convert them into soundwaves which would allow agents to 'bug' a room from the other side of a street.

A satellite system (possibly Arab-funded?) capable of changing the weather of a region, to create global droughts and then irrigating the middle east into verdant, profitable land.

A popular brand of fitness device (as used by government employee etc.,) is equipped with hidden microphones and transmitters to leak confidential conversations.

Trisha then read it a third time and thought quietly to herself – "How much of this is, or could be, real and how much is imagination? Someone here is going to need a steady head as we start serious work on all this – and I guess that is me!"

CHAPTER EIGHTEEN

The New Arrivals from Moscow

Sir Alistair arrived to start his second month in the new job, hoping for a few quiet days to settle in - especially after the challenge of moving his family belongings out of their Cheltenham house, and shipping most of their furniture into storage until they could decide on a new home in the London area.

Melanie was waiting and he was relieved when she said "nothing urgent" as she passed him a filing box full of documents. But very soon there was a knock on his door and his first caller was the ever-enthusiastic Gordon Livesey, now the acting Director of Operations. "Is this a good time for an update and some new developments?" he asked.

"Can it wait until Trisha is available," replied the new Managing Director. "In fact, I think we might try to start each week by having a meeting with you both, if we are all on base at the time of course?"

They did not have to wait more than a couple of minutes. Trisha had just arrived at her new office, via the coffee machine, and the two Directors were soon ready for their first joint briefing session with the boss. He began by saying that for starters, he wanted a summary of the main subjects on which each of his top Directors was focussing – and that this would provide a basis for his agenda at future meetings.

"I would like this to be at least a weekly arrangement," he added. "I can then follow up with you for any further information I may need for my regular Tuesday meeting with the Home Secretary. And if any of us happens to be travelling on Mondays, we can hook up by phone on the red circuit. So what have you got this week, Gordon?"

The report began by describing the arrival of two new faces from FSB at Heathrow – "We had their names from the manifest in advance as usual and neither had been to the UK before," said Gordon. "Our records showed that one was a technology expert and the other a young agent we have previously tracked on assignments in the USA and Japan. So we have put a special tracking team on them with the Met and try to discover what they are doing."

The acting Operations Director then recalled the meeting over dinner with his new boss together with his previous boss – only to suddenly remember that "it never took place". Sir Alistair quickly explained the occasion to an understanding Trisha. And so Gordon continued:

"You will remember that we talked about searching for an appropriate response to the ghastly murder of Tom and his wife – something which would seriously hurt the Russians, and Bortsov in particular. Well, over my years here and overseas in MI6 before that, I have quietly built up a small group of trusted agents and contacts around the world and we have reached out to some of them who might know ways in which the FSB group might be vulnerable. I have had some good feedback already and in particular some background on Bortsov and his family".

He then added that he has also involved Trisha is this task, to recall any information which Tom might have shared when they were working together. "Yes, he did chat about Bortsov from time to time," said Trisha. "Tom certainly regarded him as our biggest threat, now and in the future, so I will share any snippets I can recall".

"Good work, both of you," said the boss. "Keep me informed as you make more progress."

CHAPTER NINETEEN

"This is for Tom"

Later that morning, Gordon Livesey called his wife to say he would be 'working late' that night and may not get home at all – not for the first time. He cleared his in-box to deal with any immediate issues, then he checked with his operations staff on the arrangements for current monitoring activities at the Russian Embassy and was assured that everything was in place as agreed. And then he asked his communications chief to his office for an update on the assignment to research the activities and private life of the FSB chief Yuri Bortsov.

"So what more have we got," he asked Robin Sinclair, who had arrived promptly with a red filing box labelled "top secret".

"Our man at the Moscow embassy has been using his local contacts and has made a good start," began Sinclair. "Bortsov is a workaholic and spends long hours at the office. But his soft spot is his two teenage sons, now about 16 and 18, and we are building up a picture of their way of life. As well as his official home in the city, he has a dacha in the country where he usually spends family weekends. He also has an official aircraft at his disposal which the family seem to use quite freely for longer trips.

"They also go to the luxury home of a well-known banker near the Black Sea resort of Krasnodar Krai about once a month. It appears that they travel there with at least two security agents and sometimes other friends. The attraction there for the two boys seems to be their hobby of snorkelling and diving. Our research team here and in Moscow is now monitoring their movements day by day and hour by hour and we are trying to build up a pattern of activity which will help us to find a way to interrupt their comfortable life".

He added that there had also been some useful insight on Bortsov from Tom's personal files, contributed by Tasha, which could be summarised as being a "ruthless and ambitious operator".

Gordon Livesey congratulated his colleague, who then handed over a paper clip containing what he described as "the key points so far". He then surprised Sinclair by telling him that there was no time to waste and he wanted to start putting together an action plan right away. "Can we get on a safe line to the Moscow embassy before the end of their working day and talk to your best contact there who knows about all this?"

"Okay. Give me ten minutes and I will get back to you," said Sinclair who went back down to the operations centre to set up a confidential circuit for the call. When he arrived, the duty communications officer handed him a decoded message just received from his Moscow contact:

"Target plus 5 others now en route to airport – more follows".

Sinclair quickly returned to the Director's office, where Gordon Livesey was still reading the documents he had been given earlier. He handed over the brief message and told his boss, "This could be timely?"

"You bet it is, "said the Director. "Get our air traffic tracking people on to this straight away and see was they can discover about military flights from Moscow for the rest of the day. And also call your man there anyway and tell him to stand by. This may have reached an action stage more quickly than we expected. I will join you again in the operations centre when you have any more information."

Fragments of coded information began to arrive, but it was nearly an hour later when

Sinclair had a clearer picture from his contacts to report to his boss: "It appears that two women, two young men and two older men boarded the flight, but that Bortsov himself then returned from the airport in the official car and headed back to the city. The aircraft has taken off and is heading south, as we would expect. It has not registered a destination yet, but these military aircraft rarely do, and certainly not for a domestic flight".

Livesey pondered on this for a few moments as he tried to interpret this new information, together with the details in the notes he had been given earlier. The two men began to put together a possible scenario, assuming that the passengers on the aircraft were probably Bortsov's wife and perhaps a friend, together with the two boys and two security agents – "off for some recreation on the Black Sea shores again", they agreed.

They were still mulling over some remote possibilities for interrupting the flight or maybe tracking its passengers on arrival. This would not be possible at a Russian military airport, but they could possibly be tracked en route to their destination.

"How about an airstrike on their vehicle during its journey," suggested Sinclair, adding quickly: "But from where? Cyprus maybe?"

They were pondering this and other ideas when more news arrived from the aircraft tracking section:

"Target flight changed course to Southeast. Leaving Russian airspace and seeking a landing slot at Sharm el Sheikh."

"This looks a lot more interesting," said Gordon Livesey immediately. "That's a Red Sea resort in Egypt and I worked in that area a few times in the past. The city is a hotbed for informants to meet up with agents from the West and from the Gulf states. Also I remember that the Red Sea coast just a few miles away has one of the world's best areas for recreational divers. There are some interesting wrecks to explore as well as marine life – probably just the place those Bortsov boys want to enjoy."

Gordon said he needed to report this new situation to the DG and asked Sinclair to call him immediately if there were any new developments. He called Sir Alistair who said he was available and after a few words about the situation he quickly decided to join the two of them in the operations centre to consider their options in detail. During the discussions that followed, Gordon said he still had at least two experienced 'underground' contacts in Egypt – one in Cairo, and the other last heard of in Sharm el Sheikh.

"They are experienced operators and will understand the situation. I think I can track them down and work with them to decide on a plan of action. They always had great local contacts – and maybe I will travel to the Red Sea again if necessary," said Gordon, confidently and relishing a possible return to the front line.

"OK, whatever you need to do – just go for it," said Sir Alistair, giving his operations specialist a green light. "This is for Tom – so good luck," he added."

Gordon went on to work through the night, tracking down his old contacts and discovering their latest news and experiences – as well as recalling former times they had shared. One of them was a former mercenary from South Africa, now based in Cairo; the other was originally from Pakistan but was still living in Sharm el Sheihk. They fully understood the situation described by Gordon and clearly relished the challenge as he described it step by step. They also knew they would be well rewarded – "No problem" they each replied, over and over again – and the man in Cairo left at once to get the first domestic flight available to Sharm el Sheikh.

Working with their own local contacts, they knew exactly how to trace the arrival of their target group, and to discover the hotel or house where they would be staying. They also developed a plan to track their activities at whichever diving centre they had chosen.

"I have been snorkelling in that area many times", said the South African, cheerfully in one of their calls. "Actually, there are half a dozen different locations with all the facilities, and I know how it works. It is always very busy at this time of year which will help us. I know I will enjoy this one."

After several more calls during the long night, the plan was carefully agreed and Gordon ensured that they both knew how to contact him as necessary. As he finally lay down on the sofa in his office to relax at about 5am, he felt confident, but quite disappointed that he did not have an excuse to fly out to Egypt the next day.

CHAPTER TWENTY

The "New Toys"

It was at 9am when the two Directors arrived in the DG's office for a routine briefing. Gordon Chivers had freshened up and changed into the clean clothes he kept in his office for such occasions.

"Are you ok?" asked Trisha, recognising her colleague's slower than usual demeanour as they walked in together. "Just a busy time," replied Gordon, "But no problem".

The acting Director of Operations then went on to report to Sir Alistair on all the current activities of his team, both in the UK and overseas – but not mentioning his overnight challenge. He focussed on details of the round-the-clock surveillance on the Russian Embassy in London and explained: "We want to know exactly where those two new arrivals from Moscow go if they leave the embassy and we are monitoring the embassy for any clues about the use of the equipment they sneaked in. I still suspect that it could have something to do with those reports we had about the use of laser systems in Moscow?"

"That's interesting," interrupted Trisha. "You probably know that your two people from Cheltenham left me a list of new technology developments? Well, one of them described the concept of using a laser system as a listening device – which sounded ominous. Do we know any more about it?"

"Yes, I saw that list before they brought it here," replied the DG. "These are just some of the futuristic technical concepts which the researchers at GCHQ had come up with and I thought it would give you a few ideas for starters. As you said, Gordon, we have to discover whether the item about laser technology had any connection with those strange signals our satellite monitors picked up. It seemed to me that further research into this is more the province of our technical people here at MI5 rather than at GCHQ. So it is now in our court to follow up and to discover what is real?"

Gordon nodded his agreement and went on to say that this information certainly justified the decision not to detain the two new arrivals from Moscow at the airport or to confiscate the equipment at that stage. "We can now try to discover more about how their hidden equipment might be used, whatever it is. This could prove to be much more valuable than getting involved over the diplomatic bag and creating another international incident at the airport last week."

Sir Alistair said that everything pointed to the need to monitor activities at the Russian Embassy even more closely - "particularly to watch the movements of these two new arrivals and to liaise with GCHQ on any unusual communications traffic."

Gordon agreed to set up these additional measures immediately and to liaise with the Metropolitan police security section on their regular reports of activity in Kensington Palace Gardens.

He then asked to see a copy of the list which came from GCHQ. Trisha had a spare one to give him and after reading it through quickly, he responded with a gasp. "Wow - and I guess this only scratches the surface of what lies ahead for us. You are going to have an interesting time, Trisha".

She nodded her agreement and then went on to update her colleagues about her first two researchers from GCHQ, who would be joining her in the next day or two. She also told the others of her decisions regarding the two new administrative assistants starting soon "to get the show on the road." And she added that she was also looking forward to more reports about the couple from Moscow - which might add some useful information for their research on new technologies?

As their discussion went into more detail, Alistair McLaren became even more confident that his new two-division structure was starting on the right lines. "We will have another session like this in the next few days," he concluded. "And meanwhile, keep me in the picture".

Gordon returned to the operations centre to monitor progress, both in Egypt and also at London's Russian embassy, while Trisha prepared for the arrival of her new team.

First to arrive was Viraj Gupta. He arrived unexpectedly that morning and was brought up to the new offices by her temporary assistant, Jane, to announce himself enthusiastically: "Here I am, ready to go." He went on to explain that having completed his final project at GCHQ, he had already moved from Cheltenham to share an apartment in the Westminster area with a former university friend.

Jane brought them pot of coffee and as Trisha and Viraj relaxed and got to know eachother, he told her to expect his colleague Tina Heathcott to arrive in a couple of days after completing her move into a family home in West London. "She has lots of important friends," he confided.

As their conversation continued, he was introduced to Jane as the assistant who would help him to set up his office requirements in the room next door. It was explained that Jane was on temporary loan from the operations division next door, but would soon be replaced by Trisha's now permanent Personal Assistant, Victoria Browning, who currently worked in the finance department but would move to join the new Future Development Division in the next few days.

Viraj was then taken into the office area next to the Director's office where so far, there were just four desks with on-line connections. Trisha explained that this was where he and Tina would be based together with two administrative assistants she had already recruited and should be there in the next week or two.

Turning to business. Trisha continued: "I can see why the DG asked you to bring that list of new technology developments for me. It was a good introduction to our agenda over the coming months and even years and I can already see that the list will soon be getting much longer. But I can only repeat that our job will be not only to identify new technologies which may be of danger to our security, but also to establish exactly who is working on them, in which countries, and with what kind of development timetable.

"We will get down to more detailed planning when Tina is here next week, but it is good to see you so soon and obviously ready to go. I am here for any questions you may have, but meanwhile, good luck, enjoy yourself here and I will hand you over to Jane to help you settle in – and she's been here long enough to know all the answers".

Tina Heathcott arrived promptly at 9am on Monday morning. After a welcome chat over coffee, Trisha invited Viraj in from the adjoining office and told them about the two research assistants who would be joining them in the following week. She explained again her operating concept whereby she expected them both to be on travel much of the time, pursuing various leads like those in the list they had brought from GCHQ. The role of the two researchers would be to manage their travel requirements, but most importantly to create and maintain a new system of files and archive material as a completely new record of highly confidential high-tech information.

As they chatted, she was struck by the contrasting personalities of the two people who had been chosen for her by the new DG – whereas Viraj exuded energy and endless enthusiasm, Tina was calm and elegant. This is going to be an interesting time, she thought.

Jane then took the two newcomers to their office area where Viraj had already chosen the corner desk, which was looking organised and efficient. "Your turn now, Tina," she said. "Tell me and Jane what you need and we will soon have you settled in as well."

CHAPTER TWENTY-ONE

Tracking the Spies

At the MI5 control centre in Thames House, there was regular contact with two agents who had been assigned to keep watch in Kensington Palace Gardens – one was in a sports car positioned near the Russian embassy gates, and the other in a first-floor window of an elegant nearby house owned by one of Britain's royal family. They also liaised with the police control room at New Scotland Yard and recorded all the movements in and out of the embassy. In the early evening, they spotted the two target individuals who were taken by car to the nearby Royal Lancaster Hotel. Another agent was then assigned to keep watch at the hotel overnight, but there was nothing further to report.

The next morning, the two men were seen to walk back to the embassy, and a short time later there was another positive sighting, when a London taxi arrived and after a short wait, departed with them both. "They matched the description of our targets, but did not appear to be carrying any equipment," came the first report. "Our car is following and I will stay in touch."

A replacement agent in another vehicle quickly arrived on the scene and parked adjacent to one of the usual police cars from the security division. Meanwhile, the regular reports from the driver of the sports car which had followed them seemed to confirm that the new arrivals were on a sight-seeing trip which took them to the South Bank, then through Westminster and Downing Street, Trafalgar Square and eventually dropped them at the British Museum.

When these reports flowed to Gordon Livesey, he decided to stand down the monitoring team for that day and to reassess his plans. He went to update his chief and told him: "Those guys with the diplomatic bag may have been no more than couriers and there are probably more senior technical people at the Russian embassy working on the next move. But I will be sure to keep close to it any way."

"Well, stay as close as you can," said Sir Alistair. "We obviously need to see what this new equipment is and whether they start using it. But if nothing else happens, I still want to find the right opportunity to detain those two couriers for misuse of the diplomatic bag and then lodge a top level protest through the Russian Ambassador".

He went on to explain to his operations chief that he believed the two men from Moscow were likely to be involved in the actual use of the equipment, whenever it occurred. He did not think the Russians would have entrusted such a mission to anyone without the appropriate experience, especially if it was new technology unseen in use by anyone in the London embassy.

"And whatever happens, we already have the video recordings from the airport to be used as evidence for challenging their use of the diplomatic bag when the time comes", he added, "This could be become an important case with wider implications. So my instinct says that we should keep a high priority on monitoring all movements in and out of the embassy for the time being."

Sir Alistair nodded his agreement and then asked his operations chief if there was any news from Egypt? "Just a brief message of reassurance," came the reply. "It also added a word which implied action later today."

The DG said he would be patient and quietly admired the multi-tasking skills of his experienced new colleague.

As he left the meeting, Gordon Livesey was confident about the new tactics of his boss and set about revising the instructions to his security section, requiring a 24-hours team operation at the Russian embassy. The primary objective was to keep watch on the two agents who had arrived with the diplomatic bag; and also to monitor any unusual arrivals and departures and any unexpected electronic transmissions. He took the unusual step of briefing the operators personally to emphasise the important of this assignment.

CHAPTER TWENTY-TWO

Target Trafalgar Square

Ambassador Andreev called his senior team together for an early morning meeting in his elegant office suite at the Russian Embassy and told Lebedev, the FSB section leader, to bring Vasiliev and Ilia to join them.

"It did not even take 24 hours to find a suitable location for this operation," he began, proudly. "In fact, my star researcher came back to me with an excellent solution last night, but I did not want to disturb you. I got her to check a few of the facts but I think we now have an excellent solution to our technical test."

It was unusual for the Ambassador to become so personally involved in such an operation, but he was clearly enthusiastic about the potential applications it offered. He went on to explain that they had decided not to risk setting up a test at any of the government buildings in Westminster, where there would be high security. However, his researcher had found that there was to be an important private and exclusive meeting of top business executives the next day at the Canadian embassy near Trafalgar Square. And there was some evidence that a senior government officer would also be there - possibly even the prime minister.

He went on to explain that there was a major international business conference opening in London later in the week and a small group of important people from Canada and other British Commonwealth countries would be meeting at the embassy to consider a UK government proposal for new trade agreements after the withdrawal from the European Union.

"This sounded just right," he added. "And what is more, there is a hotel opposite the embassy which has rooms which overlooking the area. I don't know how she discovers these things," he added. "But she is usually right."

He went on to propose that they should immediately book two rooms at the hotel for the next three days and find two suitable couples to check in and try to discretely get at least one room with a view of Trafalgar Square. He asked Vasiliev to confirm that it was possible to set up his equipment there overnight and do any tests he needed to carry out by the next morning.

"Yes, sir - why not," came the confident reply. "We will need to find a suitable location for concealing the small transmit and receive unit. It could even be on the window ledge of the room we are using. We will be monitoring the signals from inside the hotel room and then if we have a direct line of sight, the only challenge will be to locate the room in the embassy building where the meeting takes place. Since this is just a technical test, we will not be trying to record a whole meeting so we should be able to scan the embassy one section at a time until we find a response which sounds right".

The Ambassador added confidently: "It occurs to me that you should also be able to see when the prime minister and his entourage arrives at the front of the embassy and maybe you can track them as they go inside?"

"Yes, that's very possible," replied Vasiliev, warming to the challenge ahead.

As a next stage, the other experienced agent from Moscow, Pavlov Ilia, was assigned to go to the Trafalgar Square area immediately and carry out a casual reconnaissance of the area around the Canadian embassy and the hotel opposite. He should take some photographs and return as soon as possible. Ilia called a taxi and was soon on his way with his I-phone ready.

The Ambassador decided that the next stage was to find a couple from among their staff who would be suitable to become involved in this challenging plan. He asked his two most senior diplomats to consider the challenge of accessing the hotel facilities for the technical trial and then to arrange a suitable room reservation. He added that he would then want to brief them personally on their involvement and also introduce them to Vasiliev. "Let's reconvene here in a couple of hours," he said the, ending the meeting.

The diplomats went first to the embassy's head of personnel to seek her help in identifying possible candidates who could meet the requirement for a couple to register at a central London hotel - "capable of being typical tourists, speaking and understanding English and both suitably discrete." She quickly came up with several names and produced their files to review. They picked out two, who they recognised but did not know well. One was a telecommunications expert, married to another member of the embassy staff in the archives department; the other was an experienced agent with a wife and family living in the suburbs. "Let's meet the couple who both work here first," they agreed.

Both were surprised to be called to the personnel office - and even more so when the mission was explained briefly as a requirement to pose as visitors to London and to book into a room for two at a specified hotel. They were intrigued and realised the importance of the meeting when they were told: "It starts tonight and you will be briefed personally by the Ambassador later".

CHAPTER TWENTY-THREE

Operation Laser

Igor Popov and his wife Helga had both worked at the Russia Embassy for three years. He was a technician in the telecommunications section and she was a researcher in the library. Each of them was feeling nervous to be called upstairs to the Ambassador's office; what exactly lay ahead?

"Relax", said Ambassador Andreev, as he saw their anxious expressions. "I have picked you out for a very special mission here in London tonight. You know the city well after all these years and I gather that you speak the language better than most. So what I am asking you to do is this - we will book a hotel room for you near Trafalgar Square with false names - just make sure it is a room with a window overlooking the square - and there is nothing else for you to do...."

The Ambassador paused while they looked at each other with disbelief and then he added: Well not quite.... one of our technology team from Moscow will be joining you there to carry out an experiment to spy on a building on the other side of the road. I will call him up to explain what he has in mind - okay?"

He asked his assistant to find Vasiliev and Ilia to join them and then asked the couple: "Any questions while we are waiting?"

It was Helga who answered: "Are we in any danger doing this?" she asked.

"No, no," replied the Ambassador. reassuringly. "We are only testing some interesting new equipment and no one will be in any danger. You have been here longer than me and you should know that this is a very peaceful embassy - unless we are provoked of course. I have been in lots of more dangerous places than this in my career."

When the two agents arrived, he introduced them as "two young men from Moscow who had arrived a couple of days ago on the special mission I outlined to you." He then asked Vasiliev to describe their mission in more detail.

Vasiliev began: "My team at FSB in Moscow has developed a new system which uses lasers which can penetrate walls and listen to conversations inside any building." He went on to describe the technical details and finally added: "I am sure you have been in this business long enough to know how valuable this could be?"

The couple nodded their understanding, and he continued: "We have done tests in Moscow which were successful, but we also needed to discover how easy it would be to take it to another country and use it there. The equipment is quite small and fairly easy to operate and your colleagues here have found a place for us to carry out a realistic test."

The Ambassador intervened: "Yes, we have found a hotel which is opposite an embassy building. When you are settled into your room there, you will have a visit later from Ilia, who will bring the technical equipment with him. Then Vasiliev will arrive later to meet you in the bar for a vodka or two, and then he will need to go to your room with you to set up the equipment. If it all goes to plan, he will then leave you in peace until tomorrow morning when he will return. Then when there is some activity in the building opposite, he will see if he can use the system to listen in on conversations there. And that is it. Okay?"

Igor turned to his wife, who looked worried, but she indicated her agreement. Then he told the Ambassador: "We know how important the work of FSB is to our national security of course, and all the things that they do around the world to keep us safe. So we are pleased to do our part.

Do we have time to go home first to pack an overnight bag?"

"Yes, of course," replied the Ambassador. "And we will give you the details about the hotel and the false names and home address we will use when we reserve your room. So thank you and good luck."

And with handshakes all round, the group left the top floor and went down to the offices of the FSB section for a final briefing. As they tried to relax there, Ivan Lebedev told the Popovs that a reservation had been made for them at the chosen hotel in the names of as Ivan and Helga Bridges from Sutton Coldfield, near Birmingham - and he gave them written instructions which also included their full UK address and phone number together with a credit card in their 'new' name. "I think that is all you will need," he added. "So good luck."

CHAPTER TWENTY-FOUR

Tracking the Plot

In Kensington Park Gardens, at least one vehicle from the Metropolitan Police diplomatic protection unit is always parked near the gates into the Russian Embassy, with a change every four hours. Meanwhile, on this day, a planned succession of MI5 agents also passed by the gates regularly in unmarked vehicles and maintained regular radio contact with the police officers parked there. Each time a vehicle arrived or left the embassy, one of the MI5 team was able to follow and report its location to the HQ control room.

An early morning sighting was a London taxi, which waited at the Embassy gate until it picked up one man who was photographed from the police car and was quickly identified as being one of the two who had flown into London two days earlier. Ten minutes later, a report came from Trafalgar Square, where a local police officer on regular duty was able to continue to trail the man known to be a Russian agent and to provide frequent updates....

"Target is moving around with the tourists ... taking pictures of Nelson's column ... now the

National Gallery ... now he is looking at South Africa House and then Canada House across the road ... he is taking pictures of a couple of hotels as well ... and now he is walking away down Pall Mall and hailing a taxi ....."

Gordon Livesey was in the control room listening intently and went immediately to discuss this latest information with the DG. As they studied their map of the area, they tried to interpret what may be in the Russian plans? Then came an update from Kensington Palace Gardens to say that the man who left earlier had now returned to the Embassy after an absence of only one hour.

Sir Alistair finally told his operations director: "Get your team to start checking everything happening in the Trafalgar Square area in the next couple of days. Are there any VIP visits or special events or even demonstrations, big or small. See if anyone of importance is staying at the hotels. Send a couple of your guys there straight away to ask around? There must be something happening of interest to the Ruskis. Check out everything ..."

Within 30 minutes, Gordon Livesey had most of his team focussing on the challenge without any positive results until another message came from the police car at the Russian Embassy in mid-afternoon ... "a man and a woman have just left together in a taxi and they are not people we recognise."

One of the discrete security service cars took over and followed the taxi and reported later that it had dropped the passengers at a house in the Ealing area, but the car was waiting outside. Another call ten minutes later said that the couple had left the Ealing address with a small suitcase and was now heading back into the city. There were updates on the route being taken through the afternoon traffic and finally, the couple were delivered to a hotel in Trafalgar Square. A few minutes later, two CID officers (one male, one female) from the Metropolitan police arrived at the hotel and began to make discrete inquiries in the busy lobby.

They were linked to both the Metropolitan police and MI5 control rooms, and Gordon Livesey asked them to discretely brief the hotel manager and discover the names and room number of the couple - and whether their room faced the Square?

Then came a report from the police at the Russian Embassy that the two recent new arrivals from Moscow had just left in an embassy car - which again was followed. Next came a report that it had unloaded its passengers at the same Trafalgar Square hotel. They had not been carrying any luggage - the car has waited, and they left after about 10 minutes.

And while the team at MI5 were waiting for an update, the news came from the Metropolitan police that they had just been briefed about a private visit to the Canadian embassy the next morning by two government ministers, requiring additional security.

"The plot thickens," said Gordon, who immediately went back to the top floor to report this development to his DG.

And then he added quietly: "By the way, I have just had news from Egypt – it simply reported **mission accomplished**. I will be following up with my two guys there as soon as possible, but that is all we need to know. I think we should just wait now until we hear some reactions from Moscow."

A mutual fist punch between them was all that it needed.

CHAPTER TWENTY-FIVE

Ready to Go

Ambassador Andreev went down to the FSB section at the Russian Embassy in the early evening for a briefing on the fast-developing situation from Ivan Lebedev and his team. He was told that the reconnaissance had been completed, that the two embassy staff posing as tourists were now established in a suitable room at the hotel and that Vasiliev and Ilia had also visited the location.

Vasiliev reported that the hotel room had a good view of the Canadian embassy building and that the window location was satisfactory for their mission. He suggested that he and Ilia would return again separately later in the evening, each carrying part of the necessary equipment which was small enough to be easily concealed. They would meet up with the couple from the embassy and maybe have an evening meal nearby with them before going up to their room again.

"How long will it take to set up the equipment and confirm that it is working as planned?" asked the Ambassador.

"Not long," said Vasiliev. "This version is designed to be portable and lightweight and I can be running testing operations in about ten minutes. I suggest that Ilia and I then get a cab back to our hotel in Kensington this evening, and then return to Trafalgar Square early tomorrow morning."

Lebedev said that his information suggested that the meeting they were targeting would not begin until after 9am when other participants had arrived there from different parts of the city. Also, he added, there was the rumour of a VIP from the British government also arriving at some stage to join the meeting.

"I imagine that will mean more security at the embassy," commented the Ambassador. "But the police will probably be focussing on any protesters turning up with their placards and megaphones."

The group appeared to be satisfied with the plan and as they broke up to make their preparations, the Ambassador went into Lebedev's office and quietly beckoned Ilia to follow.

"Are you ok, Ilia?" he asked the young agent. "Mr. Bortsov has told me about your special mission, so did you have your meeting in the armoury here?"

"Yes, no problem," came the confident reply. "Your man there was very helpful and you probably cannot see them, but I have a loaded slim revolver under my armpit - just here," he indicated. "And in my hip pocket is a small ricin injector, much easier if I can get close to my target. And I like the sound of protesters being outside the embassy because I can probably merge with them easily."

"So what if you get arrested by the police?" asked the Ambassador.

"Well, if I do, I know you and your legal experts here will be able to advise me," he replied. "And I hope you will get a swap organised for me after a few months, like you did for Aldanov."

The Ambassador shook his head as he heard this confident response and as they left, he told Ilia: "Well I can see why you got the job. I can only say good luck……"

CHAPTER TWENTY-SIX

Intercept – or Wait?

At the MI5 headquarters by the River Thames in the evening, the Director General called Gordon Livesey and Trisha Wells to his office and invited them to relax with a small Scotch whisky.

"As my two deputies, I want to discuss a big decision I need to make this evening", he began. "Gordon knows all about it but I think it would be a good idea to share the headlines with Trisha who will be more objective.

"So to summarise," he continued, "Two agents from Moscow flew in a couple of days ago, and we have reason to believe that they have brought the new piece of espionage equipment - and one of them posed as a courier and brought it in the diplomatic bag. From their actions today, it seems that they are targeting a private meeting of commonwealth officials tomorrow morning at the Canadian Embassy. A couple of our government ministers will probably be there so there will be high level security.

"We believe that the Russian embassy has now based a couple of their people as tourists in a room at the hotel opposite the entrance to the

Canadian embassy and it is not difficult to guess what they have in mind.

"I think we have three options - one is to arrest the couple staying at the hotel tonight and upset their plan - but this would give the others involved the possibility of going into hiding and then disappearing with their new equipment. The second is to raid the hotel at about 8am tomorrow and hope to interrupt their operation and the agents before they can take any action. The third is to inform the Met about the threat and get them to arrange for all the VIP's to arrive at the Canadian embassy discretely by a rear entrance and so deprive the Ruskies of their target. OK so far, Trisha?"

She indicated her understanding so far, and the DG then continued:

"But there is another issue, possibly a bigger one in the end. This is their use of the diplomatic bag to bring their new equipment in. This is a clear contravention of the rules and I have discussed the matter with our lawyers and we are ready to make a protest. Whatever else we do now, we also have the evidence from some secret scans carried out by the security people at Heathrow – which is also contrary to the diplomatic bag rules. So I think we also need to get our hands on the actual hardware to be sure it matches our scans. If we act too soon, they may be able to contest our claim of illegal use of the bag and then keep the equipment under wraps at the embassy."

Both Gordon and Tasha indicated that they did not know enough about the rules governing diplomatic bags. So the DG explained that the system had been approved at the Vienna Convention on Diplomatic Relations in 1961 and such bags, properly locked and identified, are protected by diplomatic immunity and cannot be searched, seized or opened by customs. They are meant to convey official correspondence and items between a ministry and its overseas offices.

"However", he continued, "There have been many examples of attempts to mis-use the system. These range from carrying drugs, gold bars and jewellery to an unsuccessful effort 20 year ago by Nigeria to repatriate a wanted ex-minister from London. He was drugged and concealed in a crate identified as a diplomatic bag. This crazy scheme was successfully intercepted at the airport. But the outcome was that diplomatic relations between Britain and Nigeria broke down for two years".

Tasha asked what would be the outcome of an official British complaint to Russia? Sir Alistair said their lawyers could expect some lengthy exchanges with charges and counter-charges back and forth, and also lots of publicity which would be embarrassing to Russia - "but not much more."

Then he went on to discuss the next stages and told Tasha that he wanted her to represent the agency in the important future meetings which would take place with the Foreign Office on this breach of the diplomatic bag system.

"This is not the first time a serious mis-use has been discovered," he said. "And there are no doubt other examples around the world which have been kept quiet. So I want us to drive a new programme to reassess the existing system and to work with the lawyers on how to improve it".

"Why me and not our lawyers," asked Tasha.

"The world is changing," explained the DG. "And I believe that the future solution may be found among your new technologies. This would be a better way forward instead of having the lawyers arguing over the small print".

Tasha still looked quizzical at first, but the DG reassured her by emphasising that although it was an international and legalistic matter, this current issue illustrated how it was also crucial to security and that it was MI5 and the other agencies like the CIA which needed to take the lead.

"Get the Americans involved too," he added. "Gordon will share the key contacts with you. This issue will not arise for a few weeks yet, but give it some thought together with your new team and we will discuss it again later."

The top MI5 trio then returned to the current challenge of the equipment which had been smuggled into the country by this route. And after further discussions, they agreed that the best option would be to watch the arrivals and departures at the hotel overnight, and then send in the police team the next morning when they would expect to find all the culprits ready to start their operation - "whatever it might be".

CHAPTER TWENTY-SEVEN

The Hit

Vasiliev and Ilia returned to their hotel to rest and prepare for an important day ahead. They were joined briefly by the FSB bureau chief Lebedev, who arrived in an embassy car to meet them in the bar and deliver the two small bags containing the laser equipment. They ordered vodkas and found a discrete corner table where he suggested that they should go to Trafalgar Square independently by taxis at around 7am, taking one bag each. He had arranged for the couple staying there to be in the breakfast room - and from there, they would all find a convenient time to go quietly up to their room. He suggested that this should be before 8am to set up the equipment and prepare for the planned operation.

"Keep in touch with me on my red line," he told them. "And if you need any help, I will be standing by with a car ready to come and join you and then bring you back to the embassy."

They clicked glasses with a second vodka, and Lebedev wished them good luck before he departed.

His moves that evening had been closely followed by the police security team and reported to the control rooms at New Scotland Yard and MI5. And just before 7am the next morning, they were able to report that each of the men had in turn come outside to hail a taxi and make separate departures. The roads into the West End were already busy, but the police cars were again able to follow them and report their arrival at the Trafalgar Square hotel.

A female detective having a light, 7am breakfast at the hotel was able to report their arrivals, each of them with a small carrier bag. She saw them joining a couple already there having coffee and just ten minutes later, she was able to give the signal that all four had gone to wait for the lift to the upper floors.

This was the cue which the Operations Room at New Scotland Yard was waiting for - and a few minutes later, two police cars and two police vans arrived at the hotel to the alarm of the staff, the guests and the passing public. As guards took their places to secure at all the doors, front and rear, the armed 'hit squad' divided into two groups - three went up the stairs and three more took the lift, to arrive silently in the corridor at room 230. They could just hear the Russian conversations inside.

Igor and Helga Popov were relaxing on the double bed, intrigued as they watched Vasiliev and Ilia installing the technical unit on the ledge of the open window at the front of their room. They worked quietly as they connected various cables and did some tests until Vasiliev sat back and called out "eureka - it works" ...

Suddenly, the bedroom door was smashed open and helmeted police officers, with guns at the ready, shattered the quiet hotel with shouts of "Police - hands up - lie down - don't touch anything....."

In less than a minute, all four had been handcuffed and searched - and they quickly discovered the two small handguns concealed by Ilia. The leader reported "all safe" on his telephone and two detectives immediately arrived in the crowded room to begin examining the equipment in the window. After one had checked it carefully, wearing gloves to protect any fingerprints, they placed each of the technical units into padded evidence boxes and, watched by a shocked Vasiliev, they took it away.

Then, as guests in the adjoining rooms came out into the corridors to see what was happening, the four handcuffed individuals were led out and taken down the stairs and out to the waiting police vehicles, watched by inquisitive crowds.

They saw two hand-cuffed men - Vasiliev and Ilia - taken away speedily in separate vehicles with motor cycle escorts; and then another man and woman, the Popovs, were driven away in the back of separate police cars.

Within 10 minutes the hotel was back to normality, and the people in the area were surprised to see a strong police presence gathering at the doors of Canada House on the opposite side of the road. News cameramen and reporters were also there - but they had just missed an opportunity to cover the event at the hotel. Someone in the crowd asked what was going on - and was surprised to be told by one of the news team: "There is a rumour that the Prime Minister is arriving here at any minute...."

By then, Vasiliev and Ilia were already well on the way to the high security detention centre in south London, closely guarded by armed officers. There they were formally charged to await trial for a range of espionage activities. The Popovs were taken by car to the nearby Metropolitan Police HQ at New Scotland Yard for further questioning.

At about the same time, a group of official cars drew up at Canada House ... and it was indeed the Prime Minister who emerged to stand on the Embassy steps to acknowledge the cheering crowd, including those watching from the hotel windows on the opposite side of the road.

CHAPTER TWENTY-EIGHT

Revenge in Egypt

Yuri Bortsov never saw the urgent and confidential message to his office in Moscow from the Russian Ambassador in London. This would have informed him that his two agents, Vasiliev and Ilia, had been arrested by the British security services, together with the two Embassy staff who had been with them. It added that the mission to test the new equipment had failed and the laser unit was now in the hands of the British.

The news quickly reached the Defence Minister together with the surprise information that Bortsov had reportedly flown out of the nearby military airport an hour earlier. "Where is he going? Get me more information now," he insisted to his deputy. "And find out more about Bortsov's part in this?"

But by then, the chief of FSB was already halfway across the Mediterranean on his way to Egypt after receiving an urgent message that his family had been the targets for a terrorist attack and that at least two of them were seriously injured. More details emerged as the military plane made the 3-hours flight to Sharm el Sheikh on the Red Sea peninsular.

More information reached him in stages and he was alarmed to hear that his two sons were in hospital, together with one of their protection officers, but the other three members of the group, including his wife, were safe.

The Russian ambassador in Cairo had been officially advised in advance as usual about the arrival of Yuri Bortsov's family members from Moscow. Not for the first time, they had planned to stay a week at the luxury villa of a Russian oil magnate near the Red Sea resort of Sharm el Sheikh.

The ambassador was alarmed when he received an urgent message from his FRS security section chief about a "terrorist attack" on the Bortsov family. Then another message advised him that Bortsov himself was already in the air, en route to the resort and he immediately ordered the Cairo-based FRS chief to fly to Sharm el Sheikh to meet the Director's flight.

Meanwhile, the Ambassador also contacted their locally-based contacts in Sharm el Sheikh to discover more details.

He soon learned much more and was horrified to discover that the Bortsov sons had been there, with two security men, to be trained in scuba diving. That morning, with one of their escorts, they had boarded a boat taking a small group into a nearby area favoured by underwater swimmers to explore sunken wrecks. The group was already in the sea with an instructor when their boat was rammed and in the confusion that followed, two men in frogman suits dived into the water from another boat and apparently located the three Russians.

Other boats had quickly arrived on the scene, followed by a police boat and other helpers. And in the confusion of the rescue melee that followed, the two boys were brought to the surface and lifted into their boat. Both were unconscious and the experienced rescuers quickly saw that tubes connecting their face masks to the oxygen cylinders on their backs appeared to have been severed. Their security man was also injured and was conscious but bleeding from a shoulder wound. The two officers in the police boat began to provide first aid help as they sped back to the shore and radioed for urgent medical help to meet them at the nearest quay.

Another fast motorboat had also arrived among those in the confused emergency scene and it was seen by witnesses to pick up two frogmen and then speed away northwards into the busy Red Sea shipping area. An immediate SOS message was sent out by the police describing the vessel as it disappeared into the distance.

Attention had focussed on the three victims and ambulances were waiting on the quayside some 400 metres away where medical staff attended to their immediate needs and then rushed them to the city hospital emergency department. The police officers began to take details from those who had witnessed the attack, from on board the many boats and on the quayside. They also secured the two boats involved for close examination as well as the scuba gear which the victims had been wearing. |But the power boat which had sped away was never located or identified.

When Yuri Bortsov arrived at the hospital together with the diplomat from Cairo, his wife was also there with her friends and the news was bad. The older boy had suffered from sea water in his lungs and had died of drowning; the younger boy was still receiving treatment for lung recovery and had also sustained a serious knife wound to his back. The security man was conscious but he had been stabbed at least twice. He was able to tell the police that the attackers appeared to be armed only with large knives and clearly knew how to inflict the greatest damage in the underwater location in the fastest possible time. "It all seemed to happen in a flash," he explained. "Nothing was said by them that I could hear of course, so I had no way to recognise their nationality".

Bortsov and his wife heard the tragic details as they sat by their younger son's bedside – and all that a shattered father could say, over and over again, was "This is too much, this is too much."

EPITAPH

** A depressed and forever chastened Yuri Bortsov never returned to his office at the FSB headquarters. He and his wife flew back to Moscow with the body of their older son and at the quiet funeral with family and close friends near his country dacha, there was no one present from the agency he had led for more than five years. He had already submitted his resignation and a new Director was appointed quickly, without making any reference to Bortsov. But he was privately admonished in the Government records for his "reckless mission to London".

** "This is too much," Bortsov repeated to himself as he mourned his son and heir. After the funeral, he flew back to Egypt, this time on a commercial flight. He stayed for another two months while his younger son recovered, but with permanent scars and weaknesses resulting from the injuries he had sustained.

** In London, the four Russians were eventually convicted of a range of espionage charges and were sentenced to serve jail terms ranging from two years for the Popov couple for 'aiding and abetting' the Trafalgar Square plan; five years for Vasiliev for illegal entry, smuggling technical equipment into the UK and planning an illegal action at the Canadian Embassy; and 10 years for Ilia, for the same offences as well as carrying offensive weapons with intent to kill or injure British citizens. They all remain in jail, in spite of appeals and protests, and none of them has yet been the subject of a spy exchange arrangement with the Russian Government. However, there have been 'reprisal' activities by FSB against British interests in various parts of the world.

** The technical experts at MI5 inspected the laser equipment recovered by the police at the hotel and then called in specialists from a research laboratory in Cambridge to discover its operating system and functions. They eventually concluded that the technology had been cleverly adapted to provide a laser beam which could carry sound signals and even penetrate barriers such as walls. They soon produced their own superior version.

** At his next routine meeting with the Home Secretary and other government officials, the MI5 Director General Sir Alistair McLean was congratulated on the successful operation at the London hotel. He also reported briefly on the surprise departure of Russia's FSB chief

Bortsov. The DG then went on to describe his plan for a new division at the agency which would focus on the development of new technologies and obtained approval for this important organisational change.

** The new director at MI5, Patricia (Trisha) Wells fulfilled the confidence placed in her by bringing a wide range of high technology expertise into the agency. Her new research and development team created a comprehensive archive of global information on new technologies which became accessible to all UK government departments. This technical expertise aimed to underpin the growth of the organisation into future decades.

** Meanwhile, the Russian Ambassador in London, Andreev, was summoned to the Foreign Office to receive a strongly worded complaint from the British Government for the breach of the Diplomatic Bag agreement. He was told that his diplomatic credentials were withdrawn and that he should leave the country within 14 days. This led to further accusatory exchanges between the two Government and a proposal from Britain and the USA to revise the Vienna Agreement rules - specifically by introducing severe penalties for contravention of the rules.

** Months later, the international Convention on Diplomatic Relations group meeting in Vienna reviewed the issue. They also heard a powerful presentation from MI5's Natasha Wells describing how the miniaturisation of new technology created a new problem for the system. She also described how new technology could provide an alternative and render diplomatic bags obsolete. This controversial proposal led to wide media coverage around the world, to the embarrassment of Russia.

** Legal developments followed involving many governments, which eventually took the issue to the United Nations.

And there, many months later, the matter is still seeking agreement on the exact wording of a resolution to the General Assembly which would lead to the end of the diplomatic bag system.

ABOUT THE AUTHOR

Peter Marshall was a BBC journalist who became involved in the development of satellite communications for global TV news. In his retirement, he has co-written and edited six books on the satellite and space business, two biographies and now five spy thrillers:

"The Diplomatic Bag" follows: *"The Russian Lieutenant"*, *"Beyond the Funeral"*, *"There are No Coincidences"* and *"The Bear is Stirring"*.

For more details see: www.petermarshall.uk

Printed in Great Britain
by Amazon

51775000R00095